THE APPEAL OF AN ELUSIVE VISCOUNT

USA Today Bestselling Author
HILDIE MCQUEEN

The Appeal of an Elusive Viscount

USA Today Bestselling Author
Hildie McQueen

Editor: Scott Moreland

Copyright © Hildie McQueen 2018
Print Edition
ISBN: 978-1-939356-88-8

OTHER HISTORICAL WORKS BY HILDIE MCQUEEN

CHAPTER ONE

London, England – November 1816

THE LECTURE BY the visiting philosopher was fascinating. So much so that Clara Humphries didn't mind the cramped space or the musty smell of the upstairs closet where she hid. There were murmurs of conversation as the men below discussed the lecture, signaling an intermission and she let out a sigh knowing it would be another fifteen minutes or so before the lecture began again.

The men rarely ventured upstairs to the side balcony, where the servants kept items, so she felt safe. With the cover of noise, it was possible to open the door a bit wider and stretch her legs out a bit. Hopefully, the creaky closet door would not be too loud.

Ever so slowly, she cracked the door open and took a deep breath of cleaner air. Granted, the men downstairs smoked cigars, so it wasn't exactly as clean as she would have preferred. However, it was better than the smell of the castaway items in the closet.

It was not the first time Clara had snuck into Brooks', the gentleman's club for the who's who of London society. However, it was the first time she'd been forced to hide in the closet since the lecture was so well attended.

Throats were cleared as the second portion of the lecture would commence and Clara decided it was the perfect time to emerge. If, for some reason, she were caught, she'd pretend to be lost or confused.

Men were easy to fool in her opinion. Most thought women to be simple creatures not to be taken seriously. The ploy had worked for her often. Wide eyes and a trembling bottom lip had gotten her out of trouble more times than she cared to count.

"You'd be more comfortable out here," a deep voice on the other side of the door said.

Frozen, Clara scrambled to come up with a suitable response.

"Can you not speak? Deaf perhaps?"

She considered both. However, neither would make sense. Someone could recognize her and know she was not deaf and could definitely speak.

Clara opened the door just a hair wider and then peeked out to find the hallway to be empty to her right. Taking a half-step forward, she inched another step to look around the door to the opposite side.

A man she'd never seen before stood immobile, his broad shoulders blocking anything else from sight. He wore black from head to toe, reminding her of a dark prince from fairy tales she made up when she was bored.

Midnight black hair fell in waves to his shoulders. It was left loose and not pulled back into a queue, as was the current style.

Narrowing her eyes, she assessed what ploy to use. He didn't seem particularly put out at her being in the club. Neither did he seem pleased. If she were to be honest, she couldn't figure out what he thought by his blank expression.

She'd wait for him to speak first. While waiting, she studied the man further.

He was handsome beyond words, with olive skin, long-lashed, gray eyes, and a closely trimmed mustache and beard. Again, not adhering to the current clean-shaven look London men preferred.

"Why were you in the closet?" He finally spoke, seeming more curious than angry.

Clara placed her index finger over her lips signaling for him to lower his voice. And then with a toss of her curls, she stood tall. "My uncle is here somewhere and I'm afraid for his health and need to keep an eye on him." The whispered lie flowed easily.

He cocked his head to the side and then frowned. "From inside a closet?"

"I – I was afraid of being caught." Willing tears, Clara pushed her bottom lip out.

The man looked toward the edge of the balcony. "Who is your uncle? I'd be happy to ensure he is well and return promptly with word."

"No need." Her words came out sharper than intended. "I just checked and he seems fine."

This time, his gray eyes narrowed. "If you are certain, then you should leave. I will ensure your uncle is well."

The philosopher began speaking about the precise subject she'd read about and was most interested in. She strained to listen, ignoring the meddlesome man for a moment.

How could she get rid of the black prince and hear the rest of the lecture? She let out a soft sigh and leaned forward so he could hear her words clearly. "Allow me to remain. I will slip away as soon as the lecture ends."

"Ah, so it's the lecture that interests you then?" Once

again, he spoke without lowering his voice and Clara winced.

"Must you speak so loudly?" she hissed.

His gaze raked over her, from her head to her toes. It was as if he was assessing what to do. "Very well, remain. I will accompany you." Taking Clara by the hand, he led her to two chairs.

"What are you doing, Sir?" She snatched her hand away as if burned. "I can't remain out in the open. Being found out would be my ruin."

The man's lips twitched in amusement as he lifted and lowered a shoulder. "I'm sure it's not as serious as that."

This time, it was her that grabbed at his arm. She raced to the closet, hurried inside and tugged him in behind her. Footsteps and voices neared. Two men conversed as they walked past.

What had been a cramped space was now miniscule. Their bodies were so close they touched and his breath fanned across Clara's face.

"You almost got me caught," Clara whispered, wishing she could stomp on one of his feet. However, if he cried out, she'd definitely be discovered. Then again, the stranger didn't seem the type to "cry out".

Once again, it was quiet in the hallway. She strained to listen. Once she was sure it was safe, she looked up at her closet companion. "You can go now."

"I am rather enjoying the present predicament," the arrogant man replied, not making one single move to leave.

Clara wasn't sure what to think. Did he actually plan to remain hidden in the closet with her until it was absolutely safe to leave? This was certainly a most peculiar situation. "It's quite smelly in here. Offensive really."

For a moment, he didn't stir and then it was obvious he

sniffed her. "Thankfully, your perfume helps. Although, I must say, the musty odor does remind me of my Uncle Theodor. He always smelled as if he was just let out of the attic."

Unable to help it, Clara giggled. "We will be caught and you, Sir, will be responsible for my ruin. Please go." She gave him a firm shove. Given the cramped space, there wasn't room for him to move at all.

"Very well. I will take my leave. However, it will cost you." At his deep voice next to her ear, a tingle traveled down the back of her neck. It wasn't an unpleasant sensation.

Quite the opposite unfortunately.

What would he request? Clara did a quick calculation of how much she carried in her purse. The man had to be wealthy by the make of his clothing. "I don't have much money with me, but you are welcome to take it all."

She maneuvered sideways and dipped down to retrieve her reticule. The throat clearing made her freeze just as her face was at the stranger's crotch level. Someone walked outside. Clara held her breath her face blazing at the unfortunate position she found herself in.

"Ah, there you are, Albert," the man out in the hallway said. And after another greeting, they walked off.

The dark prince took her by the shoulders and pulled Clara to standing upright. "I don't want money. Just a kiss."

"A...a kiss?"

"Yes."

"Oh." That was silly. Why would he wish for a kiss from her? No matter. It would be best to kiss the man and send him on his way.

Clara stood on her tiptoes, cupped his jaw with both hands and pulled him down to kiss him. "Ah," she gasped when his thick arms encircled her. This was most certainly a first. The couple of times she'd been kissed, the young men had kept their hands to themselves. Their arms had most certainly not been involved.

His mouth covered hers.

The weakening of her knees and a strange, peculiar tightening of her body followed a soft moan. Clara was forced to cling to the man. Although, by the way he held her, there wasn't any chance of her collapsing, except against him.

"Goodbye," he whispered.

Clara gulped in air when her lungs protested and opened her eyes to find the closet door cracked just enough to see it was clear. Dizzy and a bit disoriented, she wobbled side to side.

In an attempt to remain upright, she grabbed at the door which, of course, opened wider.

A servant appeared at the end of the hall and Clara knew she'd been sighted. The young man hurried to her, his gaze taking in her unflattering, inexpensive dress. "What are you doing here? Are you looking for someone, Miss?"

"No…I mean yes. Not a person actually. I was told to come up and find a rag to clean up a mess." Clara smiled innocently. "No rags in there." She rushed away, leaving the befuddled servant looking into the closet.

THE HUMPHRIES ESTATE was situated just a couple blocks from Brooks'. Normally, it would be a pleasant walk. However, today, she was without an escort. If she were discovered by her parents, she'd be severely reprimanded. Clara bent her head and scurried down the side of a building hoping to reach the back gate to the gardens of her home and slip inside.

"Clara." Her father's unmistakable voice boomed out. "Stop at once."

From across the street, her father, Albert Humphries, glared at her. "What in the bloody...why are you out unescorted?" He rushed over to her, his arms pumping rather comically.

"Most troublesome as always." Her cousin, Todd, walked up to stand beside her father to form a united front of disapproval.

Straightening her shoulders, Clara prepared to perform. As if blinking away tears, she sniffed loudly. "I was out with Mrs. Tattersworth, but became distracted. And when I turned around, she was gone." She made a mental note to seek out the cook and ask her to corroborate her story.

"You're wearing a maid's outfit," her father stated flatly. "Did you also become distracted when dressing?"

Crumpets, she'd forgotten about that.

Taking her arm none too gently, her father brought her to walk beside him. "We will deal with this situation at home. Your mother will be quite cross with you."

The walk suddenly seemed much shorter. The prospect of facing her mother, after being caught out in servant's clothing and unescorted, meant hours of lectures, lessons and being forced to remain indoors.

"Father. I promise not to do this again. Please, don't tell Mother. I planned to attend the Lady's Society lecture on newly-discovered species of butterflies. It's Friday afternoon."

The lack of a response meant he would not be flexible. So she turned her attention to Todd. Her cousin was not only her father's apprentice, but also almost an exact duplicate. Tall, handsome and a bit boring. She supposed actuaries had to lack a bit of personality to be so taken by numbers.

"Dear cousin, convince Father how important it is for young people like us to have certain freedoms."

Todd shrugged. "You have more freedom that most. Why didn't you get one of the servants, perhaps the one you borrowed clothes from, to accompany you?"

She had considered it. However, it would have been difficult to sneak in with a second person. Besides, Molly would hate hiding in the closet while she listened to a philosophy lecture.

They continued on, her father never once releasing her arm until they arrived at the front door. A uniformed butler, whose eyes rounded upon spotting her, greeted them. The butler, Gerard, had been with the family for decades. Although he normally coddled her, today, his disapproving gaze moved from her outfit to where her father held her arm.

"Good afternoon. Mrs. Humphries is in the tea parlor with Miss Vivian and Miss Penelope."

"Thank you Gerard, we will join them," her father replied, tugging her as Clara did her best to dig her heels into the floor. Unfortunately, she'd not considered exchanging her soft slippers for Molly's more sturdy footwear. And so she glided across the polished floor as if on wheels.

"Come along, Clara. Best to get this over with." Her father was too strong. So, seconds later, they entered the tea parlor to meet the astounded looks of her mother and sisters.

Penelope, the youngest, coughed to cover up a giggle. Vivian, the eldest, gaped, her eyes bulging.

"What is the meaning of this?" her mother gasped, jumping to her feet. "Explain at once."

In times like these, it was best to allow someone else to speak first, so Clara looked to her father. He seemed just as terrified as she felt.

"I found Clara out near Hyde Park, unescorted and dressed in this…this…manner."

The explanation only seemed to infuriate her mother further.

"You've upset Mother," Clara informed him. "I was not unescorted. I was left behind accidentally."

By this time, her mother was close enough to pinch her. "Why are you dressed in those rags?"

The comment was rude. "Mother, you shouldn't be so judgmental. If Molly overheard you, she'd be hurt."

Sarah Humphries took a deep breath and closed her eyes. Taking advantage of that opportunity, her father dropped her arm and, along with Todd, made a quick exit.

"You will go upstairs immediately. Take a bath, put on a nightgown and go to bed. I cannot remain calm and continue to speak to you right now."

If that was to be it, her only punishment, Clara had to fight hard not to smile. "Yes, Mother." She dipped her head to seem meek and turned to leave.

"I am not finished." Her mother's words stopped her midstride. *A contradiction.* Her mother had just stated she was too angry to speak. "You will remain in your room until Friday evening. We have agreed to attend the dinner party at Lady Barrow's home. You will attend and be on your best behavior."

At the sentence, she gasped and looked past her mother to her sisters. Surely one of them would plead for leniency. Both sat with rounded eyes and mouths open.

It was only Monday. Their mother rarely punished Clara for longer than two days.

"Mother, it is impossible to remain in my room for four

long days. Whatever shall I do?"

Her mother closed the distance until their noses were but an inch apart. "Not be abducted. Not be ruined in the eyes of society and also casting your shadow of ruin over your sisters. This is Vivian's year. I will not allow you to ruin it."

"I thought you said all three of us would be seeking husbands," Penelope interjected, her hand shooting up as if asking for permission to speak after the fact.

Her mother whirled and Penelope shrank back, her eyes rounded. "I mean…of course Vivian should receive all the attention. She is, after all, the eldest and soon will be considered a spinster."

"Penelope!" Vivian cried out. "I have at least another season before that could happen. I am only twenty-one."

Her mother placed two fingers on both temples. "Enough girls. We will adjourn to Clara's room after tea and discuss the season." She looked to Clara. "Go to your room now."

"About Friday…" Clara started.

"I could change it to Saturday. You'd go straight to your room after Lady Barrow's party."

CHAPTER TWO

T HE CITY TOWNHOME was large enough. However, in William Torrington's opinion, it needed less furniture and more windows. He stormed from the front door, a footman on his heels.

"My Lord, I wasn't aware your hounds would not heel when commanded. They bounded across the park and disappeared into the streets beyond. I've spent hours searching for them."

William took a deep breath and curled his hands into fists. Damnation, if the dogs were lost, he'd kill the idiot. The dogs were more than just pets. They were his family. Those dogs were the only companions he kept while living at Lark's Song, his country estate. "Why did you not keep them on leads?"

"Mister Yarnsby ensured me they were very well trained. I kept them tied until arriving at the park. I then thought they'd enjoy a good run." To his credit, the young footman looked about to dissolve into tears.

"Where is Alexander?" he asked, inquiring about his friend who'd just arrived the night before from Berkhamsted, where they both lived.

"He's gone to the tailor, My Lord."

"Saddle my horse and bring it around. I will change momentarily and go in search of my dogs." He glared at the now pale footman. "You best pray I find them."

THE RIDE TO Hyde Park was not long, thankfully. Although the weather remained chilly, it was also uncharacteristically sunny. Taking advantage of the unseasonably mild day, there were plenty of people out riding or strolling at the park.

William caught sight of his friend. The man being flanked by three women meant the usually quiet man had been ambushed. Normally, he would have ignored what was happening just to chide Alexander later about the situation. But on this day, help was needed to find the hounds.

The look of relief on Alexander's face was comical. "Ladies, may I present Viscount William Torrington, my childhood friend from Berkhamsted?" Alexander continued by introducing the women, one by one, as each nodded and he returned the gesture.

"Mrs. Verna Smiting, and her daughters, Irene and Willa," Alexander pronounced, his voice smooth, but flat. It was a tone William recognized to mean he was not at all interested in either of the daughters.

Three calculating gazes raked over him, assessing his worth no doubt. The first woman to respond was Mrs. Smiting.

"My Lord, I hope you will be in attendance at the holiday galas this season," the woman purred. "My daughters will be available to introduce you to others in their circle as we are invited to most functions."

It would be impossible for the two younger women to bob their heads any faster. By his calculation, they would be a constant if and when he attended any function. "I do appreciate it."

Behind them, Alexander slowly slid his index finger across his throat.

"Ladies, I must beg your forgiveness for my abruptness. My two hounds are loose and I must find them immediately before they fall into mischief. I am forced to bring Alexander along to assist me in finding them."

It was an excruciating ten minutes before they were able to tear themselves away. The older woman attempted to seek information on their plans. Neither had any as of yet, so Mrs. Smiting took it upon herself to garner invitations listing each event and promising to ensure invites were delivered promptly.

Finally, Alexander managed to interrupt the woman. "Have a pleasant day ladies."

"How in the devil did you find yourself in the company of those women? You only arrived last evening," William grumbled.

Alexander huffed. "I came out to see about your dogs. I knew you'd come close to murder if you found them to be missing."

With a look over his shoulder, his friend assured himself they were not within earshot. "The mother accosted me. It seems news about our coming to London has reached the ears of every prominent household."

"Ugh," William grunted. "My mother will be ecstatic. Perhaps, it was her that sent out missives."

Shouts accompanied by barks sounded. A man wearing a white apron ran after two flashes of red fur. "Oh no," William groaned, giving Alexander a resigned look. "This is going to cost a bit of coin."

Thinking it a game, Ellington and Farnsworth, his rambunctious dogs, ran in circles. Both had a grand time eluding the red-faced man's attempts to grab them. Every so often, one or the other would turn to face the man, butt lifted in the air, as they egged him on to attempt to catch them.

With happy, wagging tails, they never got too far ahead of the man. The dogs seemed to know it would be nearly impossible for the now-winded baker to catch them.

"I supposed it's best I claim the delinquents before they are locked up for theft." Once he handed the horse's reins to Alexander, William raced to get his dogs' attention.

When he whistled, the dogs stopped in their tracks, but only for a second. Letting out happy barks, Ellington dropped his prize and both dogs raced directly toward him, right through a puddle the size of a small pond.

William did his best to avoid the inevitable by running in circles. But the dogs were much faster and, seconds later, the dogs corralled him.

"Sit. Sit. Back." William held both hands up in the hopes that their training would take over the dogs' exuberance.

It didn't.

There was a collective gasp by bystanders and everyone gaped in astonishment when William fell back into the muddy water, his dogs happily joining him, thinking it a great game.

Alexander laughed so hard he was bent forward at the waist. "I would...offer...to help..." his best friend could barely speak, so he just pointed at the horse. "Horse."

William sat up, doing his best to keep from cursing. Teeth gritted, he held both dogs' collars as the happy animals took turns licking his face. "The horse won't go anywhere, come take one of them," he snapped.

Of course, his friend ignored him. Instead, Alexander

turned to the baker. "I do apologize for my friend's unruly hounds. How much do we owe you, Sir?"

While Alexander paid the baker twice what was quoted, William managed to get to his feet while containing the overly-excited dogs. He'd have to walk back with the hounds on leads since he was sure Alexander would refuse the task.

Shaking mud off his pants and shoes as best he could, William peered down at his dogs. "Bad," he scolded them. "Bad dogs."

Both stared up at him with confused expressions. Farnsworth tilted his head to the side as if considering his words.

"Never mind."

Bright color caught his attention and he stopped to watch as three women exited a dress shop. Two women and a maid stopped just outside a shop. Both of the women's hair color caught his attention. The color reminded him of the woman he'd met at the club. Neither faced him, so he could not see if one was, indeed, the woman.

The need to know if it was, indeed, the woman he'd met the night before overrode consideration of his appearance. The hounds on leads now, he guided the dogs to walk on the street closest to the dress shop. When he walked past, he cast a glance out of the corner of his eyes.

Gasps sounded at his appearance and a bright-eyed younger version of the woman he'd kissed looked him up and down. She threw her head back and laughed, only to be elbowed by the other woman, probably her sister by the resemblance. "Penelope, you're being rude."

He continued on. It was not exactly the time to attempt to make their acquaintance in his current state.

By the time he arrived at the townhouse, he was shivering. Teeth chattering from the cold air and wet clothing, he hurried up the steps only to be stopped by the butler.

"My Lord, I can't possible allow you to enter in that state. It would be best if you go around to the kitchen entrance." The older man, Charles, lifted both brows as he blocked the door from either him or the hounds entering.

Indeed, his mother would be most upset if he allowed mud on her precious rugs.

"Very well," he grumbled, tugging the dogs back down the front steps and then along the side of the house. "Both of you are more trouble than you're worth. I am sending you back to the country where you can continue to behave like wild beasts."

The cook and her assistant both stared at him with mouths wide when he and the dogs entered and hurried to the fireplace.

"My Lord. What happened?" Fern, the cook, rushed to him with a small towel. "You must undress at once before you catch your death." She turned to the younger woman who'd yet to move. "Go see about a bath. Call Liam to come and collect the dogs."

It was good to have competent staff, William acknowledged. At his country estate, the only other person there a cook who was married to the man who worked at the stable. They looked after the estate. The wife would ensure he ate and the man helped with horses and such. However, he didn't have a proper staff and often had to hire someone to come every so often to tidy up the place. Or he did it himself.

Although he preferred a solitary life, he allowed Fern to spoil him this once. He was quickly undressed and wrapped in a warm blanket as his bath was prepared.

The footman went off with the dogs. They seemed happy to see the man since William was apparently not providing entertainment for them any longer.

An hour later, William sat in the front room, a glass of brandy in one hand allowing the heat of the fireplace to dry his still damp hair.

"It seems Mrs. Smiting has some influence as three invitations have already arrived." Alexander all but rolled his eyes. "They are addressed to us both."

There was the fact that he'd promised his mother to accept as many invitations as possible and not leave London until he found a wife. William could not help but groan.

"Have I told you how much I detest all the pretense that occurs at these events? All the groveling and fakeness just to garner invitations. People spend so much money and countless hours primping only to spend an evening in hot rooms drinking tepid punch."

Alexander nodded. "Don't forget the forced conversations as each tries to prove how much more they know about every subject." His friend lifted his nose in the air. "Have I mentioned, My Lord, how I once defeated a boar with my bare hands?"

"No," William quipped back. "I'm sure it was formidable. However, I once brought down a lion with but a stern look."

"My Lord," Charles said as he entered the room holding a small silver tray. "This came for you."

"Another invitation?" He didn't reach for the envelope. "Put it with the others please."

"The messenger is waiting your response. It seems the soiree is tonight." Charles lowered the tray closer.

He took the dainty envelope and opened it. It was an invitation to a small dinner party at Lord and Lady Barrows' home. He'd made the couple's acquaintance several times, as they were friends of his parents. Thankfully, the couple was not as pretentious as others. Secondly, it was a dinner party, which meant a smaller group. If the Barrows had young women in attendance, it meant they were in their good graces. He trusted their judgment more than most.

William picked up the quill Charles had graciously provided and scribbled a note of acceptance.

"So?" Alexander asked. "Shouldn't I know what you wrote since the invitation was for us both."

It had been a long day. William considered that, perhaps, he should have bowed out of the dinner invite, citing a cold. It was possible he'd be sick in a few hours.

"We're going. Mother would be very cross at us if we turned down her friend's invitation. Besides, it's a dinner party and will be small. Best to get some of these social obligations over with." He stood and went to a side table.

"Shall we proceed to choose which we will accept?"

Alexander let out a sigh. "I am not here to attend social functions, but to meet with actuaries about my late father's estate. Thankfully, I have a good excuse to not attend most."

William decided that if he was to be tormented by London society, so would Alexander. "You must come with me tonight. It's best to get this one over with. You will ensure everyone is aware you are here to conduct business, which will give you an excuse for future absences."

"And you?" His friend lifted a brow, knowing William would capitalize on making up a reason for future absences as well.

"I fear I'm coming down with a dreadful cold after my experience today. A well-placed cough and sneeze should allow me a reason to not attend anything for at least a week."

There was a discreet cough at the doorway. Charles looked down his nose at them, the haughty expression as familiar as the man himself. "My Lord, may I remind you that your mother asked that I travel here with you and ensure you did not come up with excuses. If you do acquire an illness after your…episode today, I will be the first to make your excuses…"

"However," William quipped.

Charles continued unabated. "However, tonight you will not display any signs of feeling unwell."

The man looked to Alexander. "Your mother wishes you to marry as well, Mr. Yarnsby. I'd hate to disappoint her with information of your refusal to attend functions held by the most elite of London's society."

Both remained silent while Charles added a log to the hearth and announced he'd see about their clothes for the dinner.

"Mother sent him along on purpose," William told Alexander who glared at the doorway. "There was nothing I could do."

Alexander let out a long sigh. "I'm sure our mothers knew Charles would be the only person who'd keep us in line."

"Indeed."

CHAPTER THREE

THE LOVELY, BUTTERY yellow gown spread out on her bed, did little to lift Clara's spirits. She'd missed not only a wonderful lecture but, according to Penelope, the most comical episode at Hyde Park earlier that day. They'd both laughed until their sides ached when Penelope had described how two unruly hounds had trounced upon a man.

The supposedly very handsome man had ended up submerged in a huge puddle and covered in mud from head to toe. Her sister had gone into great detail about how the poor man had attempted to get up several times, but his exuberant dogs had not allowed it.

Strange, and perhaps as peculiar, was that the man had not admonished the dogs, but laughed several times. Most gentlemen would have been furious at their afternoon riding clothes being ruined in such a manner.

Whoever this man was, he had a friend along that had acted as unforgivably as the hounds. According to Penelope, he did nothing to assist and had stood by laughing so hard he'd been bent at the waist.

Her sister noted that Vivian had taken notice of the friend. He was a tall, muscular man with broad shoulders, the lightest brown hair and deep green eyes.

How her sister had managed to note all of this from Minerva's dress shop to the center of the park, made little sense. However, it was interesting that Vivian took notice of a man. She was usually oblivious to the attention she attracted thanks to her beauty. Most men were hesitant to introduce themselves to Vivian, as she was quite aloof when she was approached.

Her sister was not a rude person, but instead Vivian was very shy. She was also soft spoken, but not meek, kind but fickle when it came to pronouncing a man acceptable.

It wasn't that Vivian had any reason to distrust men; it was more that she was a romantic at heart who believed in love at first sight. Now that Vivian's season in society grew near to ending without attachment to any gentleman, it was their mother who fretted.

"There will always be another season," she'd quip airily, whenever their mother stressed the importance of Vivian finding a husband.

The bedroom door opened and Penelope entered. In a violet gown that brought out her creamy complexion, her younger sister would stand out amongst her peerage. With a quick mind and a mischievous streak, Penelope cared little about proper etiquette.

She flounced onto the bed, uncaring if she crumpled her gown or Clara's for that matter.

"Get off of my dress," Clara exclaimed. "You'll crumple it and Mother will be most cross."

Penelope pouted. "Tommy isn't going tonight. I will be most bored."

"How do you know?" Clara asked of Penelope's close friend. Thomas Rutherford was a close family friend who'd had grown up with them. Tommy was now a junior Member of Parliament and quite sought after by many a young woman.

Her sister rolled onto her back and stared up at the ceiling. Clara took advantage and tugged her dress free.

"I think he wasn't invited. Why would Lady Barrow not invite him this time? He comes with us every single year." With a dramatic sigh, Penelope closed her eyes. "I should stay home."

Their mother waltzed in. Unlike them, she wore a more subdued color. Dressed in a beautiful, gray ensemble, she was regal. "What were you saying, Penelope?"

Thankfully, their mother became too preoccupied when noting her reflection in the mirror, because Penelope got away with lying across the bed fully dressed.

"I'm going to marry Tommy one day. He needs to be part of my life. It's devastating that he will not be at Lady Barrow's dinner party."

Their mother was used to Penelope's theatrics. "If you were engaged, which you are not, he would be included in the invitation. Who knows, perhaps his valor would be rewarded with his own separate invite."

"Valor?" Penelope sat up. "Goodness, Mother, you make it seem as if Tommy went to war."

"Proposing to you would be as if going to war daily. Positively exhausting," Vivian quipped as she entered the room, a delight of soft green and cream.

Despite her sour mood, Clara laughed. "Poor Penelope, you have no idea what love is. You will certainly not marry Tommy because you love him like a brother."

"I do not," Penelope protested and pouted.

Clara shrugged. "Have you kissed?"

"Clara…" Vivian gasped. "Of course they have not

kissed."

"We did so," Penelope interjected. "Right out there in our garden." She pointed to the window, her expression defiant.

Her mother shook her head. "How long ago was that?"

At the question, Penelope lost her bravado. "It doesn't matter. I'm sure if given the opportunity, we would kiss again."

"Ha!" Clara exclaimed. "You haven't had an opportunity in years then."

"Enough of this silly conversation, girls," her mother said as she made her way to the doorway. "Let us make our way downstairs. Ensure you have your gloves and cloaks. It's quite chilly out. We leave in a few moments." She turned and looked at them, her expression stern.

"It is rumored that Viscount Torrington and his friend, Alexander Yarnsby, both very eligible bachelors, will be in attendance at the dinner tonight. Ensure to be on your best behavior. Being it will be a smaller gathering, it will make for a perfect opportunity for you girls to make their acquaintances and get to know them."

Instead of going to her room to fetch necessary items, Vivian hesitated, waiting for Penelope to leave. Once their youngest sister was gone, she smiled. "Today, I saw the most handsome man. He was at Hyde Park."

"I hope he wasn't the man in the puddle Penelope told me about."

Vivian sighed. "No, he was not, but he knew the man in the puddle. He had a horse."

"Was the horse what made him handsome?" Clara giggled. "Did he introduce himself?"

"Oh no." Vivian blushed. "He was much too far away. Once his friend got out of the puddle, he mounted and left in the direction of Whites."

Clara did her best to be patient. "What did he look like, Viv?"

"Oh. Right. He is tall, with light brown hair. Interesting that he wore it loose, but then again, his hair is short. It would not allow for a queue, I suppose. I am not sure I like the look of a man's hair pulled back…"

Clara gave up on trying to get a description as Vivian droned on. Her sister could become lost in thought while talking. It was both adorable and annoying.

"Go downstairs. Mother will be calling us in a bit. I don't want to go to this dinner party with her in an annoyed mood."

Taking the gown and carefully lowering it to the floor, she stepped into it and pulled it up. It came to her shoulders, falling just enough to display only the crest of her breasts. It was a modest cut, as she hated the look of breasts about to explode over the top. After donning her cloak and gloves, Clara inspected herself in the mirror.

Her hair had been pulled up into an intricate up-do with curls falling to her shoulders and at her temples. A pearl necklace circled her neck just below the throat. She smiled at the fact her mother had not noticed she'd placed just a bit of rouge on her lips. Although she was not as beautiful as Vivian, Clara was content with being pretty. Her green eyes sparkled brightly in anticipation of finally leaving home. If this viscount was eligible, then she'd see to it that he would take notice of Vivian.

It wasn't the first time she'd played at matchmaking. Her last attempt had worked magnificently. Clara's lips curved at formulating a plan and she dashed from the room to find Penelope.

As expected, the youngest of the Humphries sisters had the smallest bedroom. However, she also had the largest collection of gowns, gloves, jewelry and accessories. Items were strewn everywhere making Clara take care when entering the room. Penelope's gaze met hers in the mirror. "I'm trying to hurry, but I changed my mind about the violet dress. I think tonight calls for a darker color, since Tommy won't be there."

Clara ignored the comment and grabbed Penelope's arm. "You must help me," she whispered.

"Help you with what?" Penelope's eyes instantly brightened.

"Ensure the very eligible viscount notices our beautiful sister. We must take every opportunity to get them together to speak. Then, once they do, we will make an excuse to leave and take whoever happens to be near with us."

Penelope clapped. "What a fabulous plan. How positively exciting." She eyed the violet dress. "Perhaps, I should wear the new gown. It will assist with my better mood."

"Girls!" their mother called out. "Come at once."

Once again, Penelope clapped, barely holding still as Clara tied her dress in the back. "Our secret code word is 'nice'. It means it is time to put our plan into action. If the plan is already in action, it will mean it's time for us to give them privacy."

"I don't think we need…"

"Girls!"

The carriage ride took half an hour and the entire way their father grumbled. Although a wealthy actuary to some of the most distinguished families in London, he would prefer not to attend functions and remain home researching. With graying temples and a riot of auburn curls that were barely contained into a queue, he remained a handsome man. "I tell you, Sarah, this is the most inopportune time for a dinner. I am on the brink of mastering the subject at hand."

"The brink can wait until tomorrow, dear," her mother replied, her face stoic. "Wasn't this the reason we missed the Rothschild's soiree last week?"

Clara did her best not to laugh when her father's eyebrows shot up. "Yes, well, and it was the reason. I am still on the same subject."

"Father, I am sure readers will love your article on socialization of criminals." Penelope attempted to make him feel better.

Instead, her father was aghast. "The article is about the reintegration into society of someone who's been captured and held prisoner."

"Oh," Penelope frowned. "That is not as interesting."

Vivian giggled and Clara elbowed her.

"Girls," their mother chided as she gave them a stern look. "Do your best to keep the conversation away from criminals or people being captured. Remain on current events in society."

Clara wasn't sure exactly what her mother meant. However, she was aware of how to hold a conversation in polite society. From the corner of her eye, she tried to read Penelope's expression. Her younger sister frowned and cocked her head to the side.

"The most intriguing event right now is the true reason why so many gentlemen meet in the library basement on Thursday nights."

"No!" their mother yelled. "Don't you dare speak about that."

"Everyone will be talking about it." Penelope crossed her arms. "I won't have anything to talk about. No one cares about the silly, old, butterfly exhibit."

"That is exactly the subject you can discuss." Their mother pressed her fingers against the bridge of her nose. "Lord, help me."

CHAPTER FOUR

THERE WERE ONLY a few other people in attendance at the Barrow's mansion when Clara and her family arrived.

The butler showed them in. "Good evening," he greeted them with a sweep of his hand, showing them in.

Clara leaned closer to get his attention. "Robert, is tonight to be an intimate gathering?"

"Depends on what you consider intimate, Miss Clara. We are expecting forty guests."

"Poo, much larger than I thought." She smiled widely at the butler who met her eyes with warmth in his gaze.

The dinner party was much larger than Clara had anticipated. That meant any plans to corral Vivian and the viscount would be tricky.

They entered into the beautiful foyer that always took her breath away. She loved Lord and Lady Barrow who, although very wealthy, were gracious to everyone regardless of social station.

Her father had been the family actuary for many years and, therefore, the Humphries were considered close friends of the Barrows.

Instead of formalities, Lady Barrow and Clara's mother hugged and kissed each other's cheeks.

Lady Barrow then hugged Clara and her sisters while exclaiming about how beautiful they were.

The Barrows' only son, Theodore, was gone to India, which meant they were free to coddle other's children. Clara didn't mind, she actually loved coming on her own on occasion to explore the couple's extensive library. After perusing to her heart's content, she'd have tea with Lady Barrow. Her visits were wonderful ways to spend a chilly afternoon.

Within the hour, the salon and parlor were filled with people. Clara sat with her sisters in the parlor, after she ensured they had a perfect view of the entry and most of the salon on the opposite side of the foyer.

Lady Barrow and their mother were seated on the left side along with Mrs. Smiting and her daughters. Clara and her sisters found the Smitings most annoying.

The woman went on and on about how she and her daughters had met both Viscount Torrington and also Mr. Yarnsby. She proclaimed them most handsome several times, which made Clara reconsider her plan to match him with Vivian.

According to Mrs. Smiting, the men had been struck speechless upon meeting her daughters. The woman's pronouncement had to be a lie, because Irene and Willa Smiting were the dullest people she'd ever met.

With constant dour expressions, they acted as if life was an ever-present annoyance.

Clara looked to the Smiting sisters now who sat side-by-side on a settee near a window. They looked straight ahead with a glass of something or other in one hand. Neither said a word, nor did they look at anyone.

"Mrs. Smiting," Clara said, getting the woman's attention. "Are Irene and Willa unwell?"

The woman swung to look at her daughters who now stared at the floor. "Goodness, no. They are so excited to be here. I could barely contain them from rushing to the carriage." After a strangled chuckle, she clapped and both daughters looked up. "It's so exciting, isn't it, girls?"

Neither responded verbally, instead they nodded in perfect time. Penelope coughed to ineffectively hide a giggle and Vivian frowned in the direction of the Smiting sisters. "I do believe Willa is ill. She seems about to faint."

"Nonsense." Mrs. Smiting, once again, looked to her daughters. It was true. Willa was pale and swayed just a bit.

Just then, there was commotion near the front door as more guests arrived. Lady Barrow got to her feet and joined her husband to greet whoever entered.

"It must mean dinner will be served shortly," Mrs. Smiting said as she jumped to her feet and rushed to stand just behind the Barrows. Irene joined her leaving Willa to continue to remain in her strange stupor.

Although it was impossible to see who entered, by the whisperings, it had to be the viscount and his friend. Several women craned their necks to get a glimpse while Mrs. Smiting's high-pitched giggle made those close to her cringe.

Penelope reached behind Vivian and pinched Clara's arm. "It would be nice if we made our way to the dining room to see who is seated where."

"Oh, yes, quite nice," Clara replied, impressed by Penelope's quick thinking. They got up and dashed away before Vivian or their mother could stop them.

In the grand room, several servants scurried about. They were busy making last minute preparations so they paid the sisters little mind.

"Here," Penelope hissed pointing at a place card. "The viscount. Oh." She pursed her lips. "It seems he is seated next to you."

Clara hurried down a few seats attempting to find Vivian's card to switch them. "I don't see Vivian."

"She's on his left," Penelope grinned. "Mr. Yarnsby is on Vivian's left."

"Should we switch them?" Clara pressed a finger to her lips.

"Why would we do that?" Penelope grabbed Clara's hand. "Who is on your right?"

She peered at the name and cringed. "Randolph Doolittle, the imp."

"That is not nice." Penelope giggled, switching the place card so that their cousin, Todd, sat on Clara's right.

"Now, let me see who sits next to me." Penelope scurried until stopping and crossing her arms. "Most horrible."

"What is, darling?" Clara neared and laughed. Gordon Barrow, the host's nephew, had been seated next to Penelope. Her sister didn't care for the young man in the least. Clara wasn't sure why, as the young man was obviously besotted with Penelope.

"You can't switch it," Clara said. "They will know."

"Crumpets," Penelope exclaimed, crossing her arms and pouting.

Clara took her arm. "Come, we have to return."

They rushed until they reached the entrance to the foyer. Then they slowed down as if they had been taking a leisurely stroll.

"There you are." Lady Barrow came to them. "You must meet my sweet friend's son. Theresa Torrington and I are distant cousins, but she is a wonderful friend who entrusted me to ensure William and Alexander are…"

Whatever Lady Barrow said faded into the background. Loud thumps echoed in her ears as she spotted him. Not the viscount, but the dark prince from Brooks'. It was as if everyone who surrounded him misted away until he alone remained in the center of the space. Commanding attention, while maintaining an aura of elusiveness, he somehow managed to be present and not altogether engaged. His gaze went from face to face as people vied for his attention.

When he bent over a woman's hand, his lips hovered but a hair above the skin. He didn't smile. But at the same time, his expression was not unfriendly. Serene would be how she'd describe him until noticing the slight tick just above his jawline.

The dark prince did not like being there. He did not like it one bit.

Although there were many guests, Clara was sure she could blend into the background so he'd not notice her. Besides, she had been dressed in Molly's dullest dress. Surely, the man would not recognize her unless they were in very close proximity.

"Come, Clara," someone said, slipping their arm through hers. Was it Penelope?

Why couldn't she hear anything? Now, her breathing came in short gasps and her lungs screamed for more air. Did she look like Willa? Was she in a stupor?

"Dear William, I must introduce you to the Humphries' other daughters. Clara and Penelope, I present Viscount William Torrington."

"How nice," Penelope quipped.

"No…no it's not," Clara said to Penelope who frowned in return.

"Clara, darling, are you unwell?" Lady Barrow tapped her cheek.

"What? Oh, yes. Yes, I am perfect." Clara lowered her head in a deep curtsy. "My Lord, nice to meet you."

"Ladies." The viscount's eyes twinkled with amusement as he bent over her hand. He did the same to Penelope, but looked to Clara. "You both look quite familiar."

Penelope giggled. "I believe I saw you chasing after your hounds at the park just yesterday. My sister, Vivian, was with me."

"I see," he replied.

"Is your friend, Mr. Alexander Yarnsby, with you?" Penelope asked searching the room.

Just as Clara took a step back hoping to escape back to the dining room to switch the place cards, said Mr. Yarnsby came to stand beside her. "I am, indeed," he replied to Penelope.

"How nice." Penelope looked to Clara, eyes sparkling. "I look forward to what this evening will bring."

Clara lifted her gaze, only to lock with the viscount's. The corners of his lips twitched and he arched a brow. He recognized her.

"Are you the quiet sister?" Mr. Yarnsby asked Clara. He was handsome and, if she were to be honest, on par with the dark prince...the viscount. However, his attractiveness was very different. Mr. Yarnsby seemed more at ease and he smiled when speaking. If there was a bit of aloofness, it was no doubt due to the fact he was unfamiliar with anyone there.

"Not at all. Vivian is the quiet, much nicer sister. She is almost without fault."

He lifted a brow. "Almost?"

"Vivian doesn't like to share her sweets," Penelope interjected. "She can be quite selfish about it."

"Penelope." Their mother came up behind Mr. Yarnsby with Vivian, who blushed at being noticed. "Come at once. I require your help in finding your father."

"This dress suits you much better," the viscount whispered to Clara. "Have you attended any more lectures?"

When she swallowed, it was a struggle. "No, I have not been allowed out of the house since that day."

"Unfortunate."

She wanted to tell him to lower his voice and not act like he knew her. But she couldn't formulate the words. Finally, an idea came to her. "My sister, Vivian, would love to tell you all about..." He was gone. She noticed him being guided away by Lord Barrow to meet a group of men.

"Good," Clara said to herself.

Vivian rushed to her and grabbed her upper arm. "Is he not the most handsome man?"

"A bit. However, I like the other one better."

"You like the viscount better?"

"No, his friend."

"That's who I spoke about." Vivian frowned at the viscount's back. "You think he's more handsome?"

"I'm confused." Clara lost track of who Vivian was talking about, her mind was bogged down with what to do about things.

"Oh, never mind."

Dinner was announced and Clara rushed to the dining room, hoping to switch the place card so that she sat next to Mr. Yarnsby and not the very distracting dark prince.

"This won't do." Todd appeared and moved his name back to where it had been originally, switching it with the annoying Mr. Doolittle's. "No offense, dear cousin, but I know you."

Clara huffed. "I prefer not to sit next to Doolittle."

"And why not?"

The man had materialized out of thin air.

Air became stuck in her throat and Clara coughed. "Nothing personal, Mr. Doolittle, my complaint is that we already know each other and I think these types of affairs are to make new acquaintances."

The man peered down at the place cards. "I've only met you once or twice." The man managed to peer down his nose at her even though he was probably the same height. "Either way, it's horrible manners to rearrange place cards." He pulled out the chair for her to sit and Clara did.

A moment later, Penelope was assisted to sit across the table. Eyes wide, her younger sister looked at Clara with expectation. "The arrangements are quiet *nice* wouldn't you agree, dear sister?" she said emphasizing the word "nice".

"Yes, they are," Clara, replied. "I expect the meal will be so as well."

It was Mr. Yarnsby and not the viscount who assisted Vivian to sit and Penelope frowned in his direction.

The moment William Torrington lowered to the chair next to Clara's, his very scent made her entire body tingle with awareness. Goodness, would people guess how he affected her? It wasn't attraction, not at all. The kiss between them had to be the reason her cheeks warmed and breathing became a struggle. It was silly that she responded that way. She'd been kissed before and, upon seeing the man again, she'd not had such a strong reaction.

It had to be that she was becoming ill. Just two days earlier, her maid, Molly, had come down with a terrible cold. Now that she considered it, she'd interacted with the maid to borrow the dress.

"Are you not hungry?" A servant held a platter in front of her. It was then Clara noted several people looking at her as if wondering if she was blind and deaf.

"Oh, goodness," Clara said, taking a small serving of meat. She gave the server a polite smile. "I do apologize."

Once the meal was served, she looked down at her plate. It held one carrot, one piece of potato and a small morsel of meat. How in the world was this going to be enough? She was positively starved. Her stomach rumbled in agreement, a mortifying hiccup followed.

"You must not be hungry," William Torrington said, noting she stared at her plate.

Clara frowned. "I am. I'm not sure why I didn't get more food."

The host announced news of a guest pianist who'd be entertaining after the meal. As everyone was distracted, Torrington's elbow nudged her arm.

He'd slipped meat and a several pieces of potato onto her plate. Keeping her head up, she peered down at her plate and then across the table to Penelope who pressed her lips together as if trying to stifle a smile. She failed miserably.

"How nice," Penelope exclaimed and waved nonchalantly toward Vivian. "Vivian is an accomplished pianist. Perhaps, you'd like to come to our home and hear for yourself, My Lord," she said to Torrington.

Vivian blushed, Mr. Yarnsby looked at the viscount and Clara held her breath.

"I'd love to hear her play."

With a wide grin, Penelope looked to their mother. "Did you hear that, Mother? Viscount Torrington would love to pay a visit."

"Of course," their mother replied with a wide smile. "I

will ensure to send you an invitation, My Lord."

"Please, call me William. In Berkhamsted, I forgo my title, which makes everyone using it here seem strange."

Penelope and her mother exchanged looks and then looked to Clara as if she should say something. Nothing came to mind. However, when the man regarded her, she cleared her throat.

"I think William is a very good name...William."

"Thank you." Thankfully, Yarnsby interjected and asked about their plans for the holidays, deftly changing the conversation away from awkwardness.

A few bites later, her meal was gone. Clara stared down at her place and then to Penelope's which remained piled with food. Her sister was not one for propriety and because of it, their mother had a constant headache. However, in this instance, the food had been so delicious that Clara wished she'd paid more attention when filling her plate.

With narrowed eyes, she slid a glance at the annoyingly distracting dark prince who spoke in quiet tones to Vivian.

When she turned to her right, Doolittle was deep in conversation with the lady to his right. This was turning out to be a boring meal.

She fidgeted in her seat until her mother gave her a pointed look. Then, leaning forward, she listened to see what both Yarnsby and Torrington spoke of with Vivian.

"I believe the ideas of society's roles for people who live in the city are quite different that those who reside in a more sparse environment," Yarnsby said. "For instance..."

Torrington turned to Clara, seeming to sense her listening in. "Do you think, Miss Humphries, that young ladies in the city are more prone to stick to the roles society has set for them?"

"Oh," she croaked and had to clear her throat. "Yes. However, to be held to certain norms dictated by others can be rather frustrating."

His eyes darkened and, for a split second, moved to her lips. "I can understand that."

"What about you, My Lord...er, William? It seems you are uncomfortable with your title. And yet, society dictates that you be addressed as such when you are here."

There was no hint of a smile. Although Clara did not know him enough to read his expressions, she'd guess the subject was something much more personal than just a title.

"I carry my title with pride. My father, the Duke of Torrington, is a great man. However, amongst those I consider friends or peers, the use of titles doesn't suit me." He lifted and lowered a wide shoulder. "It could be that I rarely find myself here in London and therefore am unused to it."

She studied him for a moment. The background faded as they regarded each other for much longer than appropriate. In her opinion, the title suited him well. Viscount was perfect for his dark features and stern personality. That he didn't seem comfortable with it only made it more suitable.

The ding of a fork against crystal caught everyone's attention and Clara quickly turned away from Torrington. At her intake of breath, Doolittle turned to her.

"I, too, am looking forward to hearing the pianist. I heard his performance was masterful when he played for King George."

Her chair was pulled back as Torrington assisted her to stand. For a moment, she wondered if he'd offer his arm since Doolittle had turned to the woman on his right and was now escorting her away.

"Miss Humphries," Torrington said, holding out his arm.

She slipped her hand through it. The contact of her hand on the fabric of his sleeve sent strange sensations up her arm.

Whatever was wrong with her? She most certainly was about to fall horribly ill.

"Have you always been prone to daydreaming?" he whispered in her ear as he led her to the ballroom.

"I believe I am coming down with a cold. My friend, Molly, is sick. I may have contracted it from her."

Distracting. He was utterly and totally distracting. It was best to tear herself away quickly and put distance between them as quickly as possible.

A servant walked by and both she and Torrington accepted a cup of punch. Clara needed more as her throat was as dry as the desert.

Penelope came to them dragging Vivian by the hand. "My Lord, you must allow Vivian to show you the gardens. The music will surely be heard from the balcony."

"Yes," Clara almost shouted. "They are most nice, even during the winter."

Their eldest sister looked to them as if they'd grown a second head. "It's positively freezing outside. I have no cloak."

"It won't take but a minute," Penelope insisted. "Isn't that right, Clara?"

Vivian looked to Torrington as if for help. "Forgive me, My Lord. It's not that I don't wish to."

Unabashed, he bowed at the waist. "I will go look at the gardens and return to hear from you all about it." He turned and walked away.

The jolt of Vivian's elbow against her waist made Clara gasp and some of her punch spilled out of her cup onto the tile flooring. At the same time, she heard a whimper from Penelope. Vivian was quiet adept at pinching and jabbing without anyone suspecting.

"Ouch," Penelope complained while she rubbed her lower arm. "How can you pinch so hard? That really hurt. I am trying hard to help you find a suitor. You should be thanking me."

Vivian glared at her sister. "You are being embarrassingly obvious. Why, even the wallpaper is aware of what you're doing. Stop it immediately."

"Oh, no. Here comes Doolittle," Penelope groaned. "The man is forever trying to get my attention."

Just then, William Torrington appeared from the balcony headed toward them. As he moved closer, Mr. Yarnsby joined him.

There was a thump as Doolittle slipped on the spilled punch. With a loud yelp, he fell to his bottom and slid feet first into Clara, causing her to fall sideways.

In a desperate attempt to keep from falling, Clara dropped her cup and grabbed Vivian's arm. Unfortunately, caught by surprise, her sister lost her balance and both sisters ended up a crumpled heap atop a very wet Randolph Doolittle.

Gasps sounded and the piano music came to an alarming stop.

The only sound in the ballroom for a moment was Penelope laughing.

CHAPTER FIVE

T HE PIANIST WAS excellent. William ended up remaining longer than he'd planned. Seated near the entrance, he was joined by Genevieve Hart, a woman with an alarmingly low-cut dress and an inviting smile. Although she was the farthest from his type, she provided a good shield against Mrs. Smiting, who'd constantly attempted to bring him into conversations with her daughters. Both young ladies seemed too glum to do more than mutter yes or no whenever he brought up a subject.

After the collapse between Doolittle and the Humphries sisters, the young women now sat between their parents, who remained with stoic expressions while listening to the music.

It had been rather comical to watch. However, he imagined the sisters were horribly embarrassed with what had transpired. Except for the youngest, whom he took a liking to, who'd giggled until she was pinched by her mother.

Clara sat ramrod straight, her hands folded over the punch stain on her gown. Although her expression was serene, it was obvious she enjoyed the music by the soft smile tugging the corner of her lips.

Those lips. The ones he'd kissed that had been so pliant against his own. Her body had been soft as well. She'd fit perfectly against his frame when she'd finally relaxed into him.

"How long will you remain in the city, My Lord?" Genevieve asked, bringing him out of musings best left for a more private time.

"I am not sure as yet. My parents come in a week and Mother has plans to attend certain events as well as entertain."

Her gaze moved to his mouth, leaving no doubt of where her thoughts were. "Perhaps you'd allow me to entertain you at my home one evening?"

The thought of a sexual affair had merit. Currently, he didn't have a mistress and a dalliance in the city was something he had planned on. However, the woman did not elicit any reaction from him. She was pleasant enough and certainly attractive. However, desirability was not there.

"I will keep it in mind, I promise," he replied noncommittally.

The woman pouted. "I hope you will."

Across the room, two women, both older and no doubt pointing out the virtues of their daughters trapped poor Yarnsby in a corner. Three younger women sat just a few feet away watching the interaction with rapt attention.

He wondered whose situation was worse, his or his best friend's. The music finally ended and the conversations became louder. William stood and leaned over Genevieve's hand. "I must find my friend, Mr. Yarnsby, and take our leave. We have an early morning appointment with the actuary." In truth, he did plan to accompany Alexander in the morning. His friend would want his opinion on how to handle certain things.

The woman nodded, her gaze already moving around the room searching the men's faces.

Loneliness was a terrible thing for some. On the other

hand, to William, being alone was what he craved. Time alone was a familiar, albeit not always welcome occurrence.

ONCE OUTSIDE THE Barrows' mansion, Alexander shook his head, looking up as their carriage was delivered. "These things never cease to surprise me," his friend said.

Settling into the plush seat, William loosened his cravat. "In what way did today's dinner surprise you? The tumbling to the floor of the Humphries sisters, or the raw desperation of the women of marriageable age who threw themselves at you?"

Alexander let out a long breath. "In truth, the women being paraded like prized horses by their mothers did not surprise me. Did you notice that Mrs. Humphries did not push her daughters to speak to us?"

"I did. They are an actuary's daughters who do not aspire to marry someone titled, I believe."

"It could be. However, it did not stop the other women there. And besides, I don't have a title."

William studied his dear friend. Alexander had lost much recently. His father died, declaring him the full heir without any instructions or information of what, exactly, was in the family's estate. The man had always remained distant from Alexander and rarely included him in any business transactions. As much as Alexander's mother had tried to bring them closer as a family, her husband insisted on keeping them at arm's length.

It had been heartbreaking for Lady Claudia Yarnsby to find out that the earl had a double life. The earl had a second family, another estate and two other children, a son and a daughter younger than Alexander. Needless to say, the earl's funeral had been a debacle of giant proportions.

Although Alexander was eligible to take his father's title, he'd decided against it. The title of earl remained unclaimed, as the other younger born son was not able to use it.

"I do believe, however," Alexander interrupted William's musings, "that the musical portion was well done. Did you and your companion enjoy it?"

William did his best not to glower. "The woman is a widow. And she was very clear that she is willing to share her bed."

"So why are you here with me?"

"Something about her made me wary. I chose to follow my intuition. It's best, sometimes, to pay attention to the head up here." He tapped his temple. "And you, anyone interesting?"

Alexander was never one to keep thoughts to himself. It was both refreshing and the reason for many a brawl between them. Since childhood, William had found himself drawn into an exchange of fists over something Alexander spouted without thought.

"I found myself enthralled by Vivian Humphries. She is open, honest and will not bite her tongue, while at the same time reserved and shy. A very interesting combination."

"It must run in the family," William replied. "Her sisters are the same, not adhering to social conventions, while never seeming to lose the ability to appear appropriate. An art form of sorts."

His friend's lips curved. "I noticed."

"MY LORD, YOUR parents have arrived." Charles greeted them at the door with a wide grin. It widened even more at his grimace.

"Thank you, Charles. I assume they've retired?" William walked into the front room and went to the sideboard to pour a brandy.

Before Charles could answer, his mother entered, her face bright with excitement. "I was so pleased to hear you attended the Barrows' dinner party. You must tell me all about it."

She allowed him to kiss her cheeks before taking his hand and tugging him to sit. "Who was there? Did the Barrows have music?"

He smiled indulgently at his mother. She beamed with excitement. Theresa Torrington looked ten years younger than her true age. She was often mistaken for being his sister and not his mother.

Part of her youthful appearance had to do with her exuberance for life. Her sparkling, hazel, almond-shaped eyes lifted at the corners. Coupled with her olive skin, her eyes gave his mother an exotic look. This night, her hair was down, unbound, flowing past her shoulders to the center of her back.

She'd often had to rush to put her hair up whenever someone visited, which the family had come to call her "hair rush".

"It was well attended," Alexander said, pouring three glasses of brandy. "The house was aglow with what had to be hundreds of candles."

As Alexander recounted the evening to his mother, William sat back, adding a comment or two.

William's mind drifted to the dinner party. The Humphries sisters were, indeed, beauties. The middle sister, Clara, had seemed nervous upon him recognizing her. Although, at first, she'd been resistant to his approach, it seemed she worried more about her mother overhearing than her sisters.

Although he'd found her pretty in the dowdy dress she'd

worn at Brooks', she'd been resplendent that night. She'd not treated him any differently than at the club, although she'd learned his name and title. That, in itself, was refreshing.

He wasn't sure if she found him appealing in any way. Most of the evening, he'd been so distracted by all the introductions and being tugged this way and that to make acquaintances, that the only time he'd been able to speak to her was at dinner. And even then, his attention had been divided between all three sisters and the every present Doolittle.

Alexander's deep voice continued on describing the music and how much everyone had enjoyed the pianist's performance.

It was endearing, the way his mother leaned forward, hands clutched as she took in every detail of the evening.

"Oh, how I wish I had arrived earlier so I could have attended," she exclaimed when Alexander described the different dessert offerings.

At the retelling of the Humphries sisters' tumble, thanks to a clumsy Randolph Doolittle, she laughed with delight.

"I remember Sarah Humphries. She is a delightful woman. Her daughters are lovely, their red hair so vibrant."

His mother hesitated for a moment. "I look forward to seeing the Humphries. As a matter of fact, I will send word with Charles that we would like to pay a visit." She covered her mouth, stifling a yawn. "Goodness, it's quite late. I should seek my bed."

After kissing them each on the cheek, she left the room.

"If all women were like your mother, life would be so much easier," Alexander said with a smile.

"True," William agreed.

THE NEXT MORNING, it was snowing. The roads were covered with a light sprinkling that always made one aware of the holiday season that approached. William and Alexander exited the actuary's offices and made their way down the street to a coffee shop.

"This weather makes me yearn to return to Berkhamsted," William grumbled. "No reason to go out other than to check on the horses."

"Even then, they are in a warm and cozy barn," Alexander added with a grimace. "The roads will soon be dirty and the air filled with the smell of burning coal."

William chuckled under his breath. "Aren't we a pair of cheerfulness?"

Just then, bright red hair caught his notice. The woman lifted the hood of a cape to cover it before darting down an alley. Whoever it was carried a basket and a small bundle.

"I'll be with you shortly," he told Alexander. "I have to see something."

"Gladly," Alexander agreed as he hurried into the coffee shop. He was too intent to drink the dark, hot liquid than to pay any attention to what he'd seen.

The slight figure moved deftly over the cobblestones until coming to a doorway. After knocking twice without answer, he or she peered through the window.

"Crumpets. Where is that boy?" It was Clara. She knocked again and the door opened. A young man, no older than fifteen if William were to guess, stepped out and dug his hands deep into his dirty pants. Hair askew, he yawned and hunched his shoulders at the cold.

Thanks to an enclave on the side of the building, William was well hidden. He peeked out to see what was happening. What in the world was the woman up to now? William was sure she'd end up in trouble sooner or later if she kept up assignations with people who lived in tiny apartments in alleyways.

"Here, take this. Make tea with the herbs and make sure your mother drinks it all. Here is some food. And this bundle holds a new shirt and pants for you." She held out the basket and bundle. "I better go now. Give your mother our best wishes."

William pushed back against the building and waited for her to come near. Just as she reached him, he took her arm.

"Ahhhhh!" Her loud scream was followed by a hard slap and a kick to his shin.

"Ouch," he yelped and released her arm.

Quick as lightning, she darted away and he gave chase.

"Clara!"

She stopped and whirled around. "What in the world are you doing skulking about in alleys?" Her eyes were bright with indignation. "How dare you scare me like that?"

There was no answer that would sound right, so he decided it was best not to reply. "I was about to have coffee with Alexander. Would you care to join us?"

"Unescorted?" She had the nerve to look down her nose at him. "Most inappropriate."

"You were just in the alley speaking to a ragamuffin. What do you call that?"

"Reaching out to the poor. Providing for those in need."

She had a point.

He arched a brow. "And your escort?"

"Mrs. Tattersworth, our cook, is at the market." She pointed to her right. "Just around the corner."

If she was lying, he wasn't going to challenge her. "It's very cold out here, Clara."

She let out a sigh. "It's not so bad. Now, if you don't mind, I'll be on my way."

Not wanting to let her leave yet, he neared. "Who was that person to you? How do you know him?"

"Jules is a chimney sweep. He comes by my home every so often to work and I've gotten to know him. He is only fourteen. Has been working and caring for his mother for years. It's a sad situation really. Every so often, I come with Mrs. Tattersworth to the market and deliver something for them."

"It's very kind of you," he replied, meaning it.

She looked past him toward the alley. "It's the right thing to do. When I can't come, I make sure someone from the household brings them food. They are desperately in need. I admire Jules for never asking for anything and always being grateful for what we give."

"I am willing to bet he is not the only person in town you help." William wasn't sure why, but upon seeing Clara with the young man, it was apparent to him that it was her nature and what she did often.

Their gazes met for a long time. Clara bit her lip as if in thought of how to reply. Finally, she shook her head. "When was the last time you helped someone in need, My Lord?"

Her question took him by surprise. As he pondered without a reply, she gave a slight nod and he touched the brim of his hat. Clara walked away to join a woman who'd been watching them from a short distance away.

INSIDE THE COFFEE shop was warm and rather crowded. The murmurs of conversations merged with the sound of spoons against the cups and plates. Alexander looked up from a newspaper when William lowered to a chair opposite him.

"Was that Clara Humphries? What was she doing out unaccompanied?"

"She was with Mrs. Tattersworth, their cook."

Alexander looked out. "Were her other sisters along?"

"Alex, do you or your mother do things for those in need?"

His friend shrugged. "Of course. It's rather a large undertaking every winter. Mother insists new blankets and food get delivered to the poor in the village. It has become a tradition of sorts. I find it..." his friend hesitated, "...a reminder of how fortunate I am to be born to a family of wealth."

"That's great," William replied considering he never took much interest in what undertakings his mother did. If she did something like Alexander's mother, he'd not paid much attention to it. Now that he lived in his own estate, he remained closed off from the local people. His cook took care of going to the nearby village for provisions. If he did go to the village, it was to visit the pub to meet Alexander and a couple of other well-to-do friends or go out for a ride.

Clara Humphries had to be one of the most interesting women he'd ever met. "I think," he began, drawing Alexander's attention, once again, away from the newspaper. "I may have just found my future wife."

"You mean the one you plan to get with child and then leave in London?" Alexander asked with obvious disapproval.

"Someone like Clara Humphries would not do well in the country. I will visit seasonally and make sure to keep her with child. I am sure that when I do spend time with her, I will not be bored."

"You make it sound so romantic and perfect. Life, my friend, cannot possibly be planned so...stringently. What if your wife were to take a lover? Long absences could make for distance between two people and resentment."

William scoffed. "I disagree. She will be cared for, provided for. She will have freedom to entertain and attend any social gathering she wishes. Besides, there will be an allotted amount of money for shopping and the ability to do all the things women like to do." He took a sip from his coffee. "If you ask me, most women would be delighted at the prospect."

Shaking his head, Alexander let out a bark of laughter that garnered the attention of customers at nearby tables. He leaned forward. "This will be a most entertaining season."

JUST AS WILLIAM was about to head up the stairs to bed, Charles appeared. "My Lord, a messenger dropped this off for you."

The envelope was crumpled, the ink on the front smeared. Whoever delivered it did not take care of it. He looked to the door. "Who brought it?"

"A street urchin. Obviously paid for bringing it. The boy could give me no name of who gave it to him."

The familiar handwriting made him cringe. A mistake from his past came back to haunt him and he decided the best course of action was to ignore the invitation.

CHAPTER SIX

THE DREARINESS OF the day seemed to seep into Clara. She couldn't shake a feeling of foreboding and it worried her. Not one to believe in such nonsense, Clara expected it was a melancholy of sorts although there was absolutely no reason for it.

She leaned back in the chaise and looked out the window to the garden. There, in the center, the fountain had remained dry as the servants had emptied it and scrubbed it clean.

Across the room at the secretary was Vivian. Quill in hand, she was hunched over parchment writing out invitations for a small tea they planned the following week. Her sister's steady hand moved across the paper, the scratching of the quill the only sound in the room.

"How many are we inviting?" Clara asked, studying the top of Vivian's head. "I hope Glenda comes. We haven't seen her in ages," she said, referring to a cousin that lived just outside London.

Vivian looked up, her eyes bright. "Mother said to invite only ten. I'm inviting fifteen." In her sister's mind, she was being rebellious.

Clara smiled indulgently in return. "How devilish of you. If all turn up, Mother will be in a tizzy."

They giggled.

The youngest sister entered and plopped most unceremoniously across a settee. "This is the most dreadfully boring day. I don't wish to study anymore and the thought of sewing or reading makes me want to cry." Adding dramatic flair, she pressed the back of one hand across her forehead. "I am in desperate need of rescue."

"It's raining, so we can't go for a walk," Clara told her sister. "Even a turn in the garden with cloaks on is out of the question."

The sound of knocks at the front door made the three sisters look up with expectancy as Gerard walked past the doorway to the entrance. There was an exchange of male voices, one being Gerard, and then the door was closed.

Penelope flew to the doorway. "Who was that? What did he want?"

Used to her curiosity, Gerard waited until Penelope tapped her foot with impatience. "Well?"

"The note is addressed to your mother."

Before he could take another step, Penelope pinched it from his hand and raced to find their mother.

Clara and Vivian exchanged looks. Then, curiosity getting the best of them, they, too, got up and followed after Penelope.

Their mother looked up as Penelope hurried forth holding a note as if it were a missive from King George himself.

"You must open it immediately, Mother. I am so bored, I am about to cry. I am hoping we are invited out to visit someone today." Penelope slapped the note against her mother's chest. "Hurry."

Sarah Humphries was overseeing the decorating of the parlor. Two servants stood holding greenery beside the large hearth. "You could be in here helping," she replied to her youngest daughter. "There is much to do and not enough time."

With slow movements, she held up the note and then looked to the servants. "Place that across the hearth and then I'll help add the dry fruit."

"Mother," Penelope started, but stopped when their mother gave her an impatient look.

Sarah went to a side table to stand beside a lamp. Then with a letter opener, she opened the envelope. As she read, her eyebrows rose until they almost disappeared under a side sweep of hair.

"My goodness."

"What?" all three sisters asked at the same time.

"Is it bad news?" Vivian asked.

"Who is it from?" Clara inquired next.

"Tell us already," Penelope snapped.

Their mother's lips curved up and she let out a long breath. "The viscount, his parents and Mr. Yarnsby are inquiring if we'd accept a visit." She waited for the full effect to sink in.

Gerard was at the door. "The messenger awaits your reply, Mrs. Humphries."

All four of them turned to the butler. Unsure what to do, he remained as still as a statue.

Their mother was the first to recover. "Yes, by all means." She hurried to the library where the girls had been with them on her heels. "I'll be but a moment."

At the secretary, she took one of the tea invitations and quickly penned a reply. She spoke as she wrote, knowing her nosy daughters would pester her to death about it. "It is an honor and we are delighted to invite you for dinner tonight.

Six o'clock. Sarah Humphries."

As Gerard walked away with the response, the girls grinned at each other as if they'd accomplished the most triumphant of things.

"Vivian, which of the two do you think will be asking for your hand?" Penelope practically swayed in delight. "You can be a viscount's wife." She danced around in a circle. "How positively romantic."

Their oldest sister frowned. "I barely spoke to either of the men."

Clara frowned. "The viscount's parents must have just arrived. It's very strange that they wish to come to visit so soon. I would say it does mean a marriage proposal." Her stomach tightened at the thought of her dark prince marrying Vivian. However, she understood. Vivian was the eldest and prettiest. At all social events, men could not keep their eyes from her beautiful sister.

The fact that William would join the family shouldn't be so hard to bear, Clara told herself. He didn't live in London. In fact, according to what she'd heard, he rarely joined his family during the holidays. Vivian and he would move away to wherever his country estate was. It was possible Clara would only see him but once or twice a year at the most. That would make it easier. Surely, the sadness that overtook her would abate by then.

It was pure folly that she could claim to feel so strongly about a man she'd only spoken to three times. And there was the kiss, the most wonderful kiss of her life.

Their mother interrupted her musings. "There is much to do. Penelope, oversee the decorating of the parlor and ensure the dining table is decorated as well. Also, ensure that fresh greenery is placed in vases."

Sarah whirled to the eldest. "Vivian, pick out the best of china and glassware. I will help you in seeing to every detail of the dinner setting is seen to."

She hesitated in thought. "Clara, choose gowns for yourself and your sisters. The dresses will need to be pressed and without any stains or tears whatsoever. Also, air out the parlor and make sure it is prepared for welcoming our guests."

The matriarch hurried toward the kitchen. "I'll speak to Mrs. Tattersworth about supper. We only have five hours, so everyone please stay on task." When she said the last words, she gave Penelope a pointed look.

"Yes, Mother," the youngest replied. Clara and Vivian were already rushing away to do what they'd been assigned.

AT HALF-PAST FOUR, their father walked in and was immediately dispatched by his wife to bathe quickly and change into dinner attire. The poor man sputtered that he was hungry and wanted a small repast or wouldn't make it until dinner, but his request was promptly ignored.

Of course, Clara could not stand the idea of her father being hungry, so she sent Molly to take tea and a few biscuits to his room.

An hour later, Clara, Vivian and Penelope sat in the parlor pretending to read while sneaking peeks either to the front door or the window. Meanwhile, their mother raced about fretting over every detail.

"We really should help. By the time our visitors arrive, she will be rendered unconscious from all this," Clara said.

"It will only annoy her for us not to do as she'd asked," Vivian replied, stretching her neck in an attempt to catch sight of Sarah, who walked by.

Penelope stood and went to the doorway. "I don't understand why Clara and I have to sit here like dolls on display when we know the only one they should be interested in is you, Vivian."

There was a light pang in her stomach, but Clara did her best to ignore it. Of course, the visit was all about Vivian. How could it not be? Her sweet and beautiful sister deserved a great match.

Finally, there was a commotion at the front door. Her parents hurried by and their mother motioned for them to line up beside them.

Gerard waited an appropriate amount of time and opened the front door wide.

There stood Viscount William Torrington, dressed all in black with a thick overcoat. Just behind him was a couple who looked to be his parents and just behind them was Alexander Yarnsby.

"Good evening My Lord." Gerard bowed slightly at the waist and motioned to her parents.

"Please, come in out of the cold," Sarah exclaimed. "We are so delighted by your visit."

The Torrington family entered. William had yet to do more than nod his head. Once they stepped inside and the door was closed behind them, he began introductions.

Clara's head swam the entire time. His father, William Delbert Torrington, an actual duke, was in her home. Lady Torrington was lovely, her bright gaze was warm when meeting hers.

Ushered into the large parlor by Gerard, everyone settled into chairs and were served brandy or tea.

Immediately, Lady Torrington began to speak. "We are grateful to be welcomed into your home on such short notice.

My son was most anxious for us to meet your beautiful daughters."

Clara's mother looked to Vivian first and then to her and Penelope. "How delightful. We so enjoyed meeting you at the Barrows' dinner," she said to William.

His dark gaze met hers for an instant. "As did I. I echo my mother's statement. You are most gracious to invite us."

Lady Torrington explained how William and Alexander were childhood friends and how they'd come to feel that Alexander was like a second son. Most of the conversation took place between the mothers, while the duke and her father looked on. Alexander Yarnsby seemed bored and William was, as usual, solemn.

"Darling, why don't you see if all is well in the kitchen?" her mother said, looking at Penelope. Seeming grateful for the reprieve, Penelope practically jumped to her feet and dashed from the room.

"There is obviously a reason for our visit," the duke spoke to the group. "It seems my son is smitten."

William scowled and let out a breath and Clara couldn't help a soft giggle. That brought him to direct a glare in her direction.

"Oh, yes," Lady Torrington exclaimed. "Son, why don't you tell them?"

He stood and went to the fireplace where her father, the duke and Todd, her cousin who'd arrived earlier, were standing.

"Sir, I'd like to request the hand of your daughter in marriage…" he continued, but the loud drumming in her ears prevented Clara from hearing more. It did affect her, more than she expected. It was so selfish, but she wanted him for herself. Vivian deserved to marry well and she hoped not to show her disappointment. However, by the way her chest constricted, it would be impossible to make it through the meal.

WHEN EVERYONE LOOKED to her, she jumped to her feet. "I think I'll see if...I forgot something. Please excuse me." She hurried out of the room. Obviously, the family wanted to discuss things with Vivian.

"May I bother you to show me your father's winter roses?" William asked as he caught up with her. In shock, she looked past him to the others in the room.

Lady Torrington was smiling while her mother seemed more confused than anything, her eyebrows lowered in a slight scowl.

Gerard provided her cloak and his overcoat and she led him through a side door to a patio.

The last thing she wanted to do was walk outside with Vivian's fiancé. Why in the world was he walking with her? She hurried to the side doors, pulled them open and motioned with both arms. "There they are. Now, if you'll excuse me."

"What is the matter with you?" he snapped. "A simple yes or no would be sufficient."

Clara looked up at him. He was so very handsome. Even the dark scowl did little to distract; if anything, it added to his appeal. The black clothes suited him so well. Her dark prince. No, he wasn't hers. "Yes or no what?"

"You didn't hear what I said in the parlor, did you?"

Unable to keep from it, she rolled her eyes. "You asked for Vivian's hand in marriage. I understand. She is beautiful, kind and will be a perfect wife. The kiss shouldn't matter." Clara looked past him toward the parlor.

"We'll keep that a secret and not tell a soul. Besides…"

His mouth covered hers and he walked her backward, outside, where no one would see them unless they were walking by.

When his large hands circled her waist and William pulled her against him, Clara was defenseless. All thought left her. The impropriety of kissing her sister's new fiancé was the only thing that finally penetrated her fogged mind. She pushed away, or tried to anyway, but the warmth of his embrace, the feel of his hard body against hers and the fact her legs could not possibly keep her upright kept her from moving.

The kiss was urgent and not gentle in the least. She wrapped her arms around his shoulders, needing more. When he slipped his tongue past her lips, a moan sounded and Clara realized she was the one who made the sound.

"Augh!" She finally managed to shove him away, although he was much too strong and his arms remained around her.

"Yes or no?" he repeated.

"You shouldn't be kissing me. My parents will throw you out. Even if you are a duke's son."

"Clara Elizabeth Humphries, will you marry me?"

"What?" she gasped. "What about Vivian?"

He closed his eyes and a rare upturn of the corners of his lips made Clara blink in disbelief. "I asked for your hand in marriage, not Vivian's."

"Oh."

Clara lowered her shoulders and, this time, firmly pushed him back. "It's most inappropriate to stand with our arms around each other. Someone might see us." She pressed her lips together to keep from grinning. "Yes."

When they reentered the parlor, William's hand on her

elbow, everyone looked at them with expectation.

Clara's first instinct was to look at Vivian. She was smiling broadly. With a breath of relief, she looked up at William.

He had the stance of a man that gave no doubt as to his standing as a member of elite society. Even if, according to everyone, he spent most of his time at a country estate, William fit into the role of viscount well.

"Clara has accepted my proposal. She will marry me."

Her mother jumped to her feet and dashed to them, her eyes shining with unshed tears. "Goodness, this is so unexpected. I am so very pleased."

Champagne was brought and served and everyone toasted to the upcoming nuptials. The entire time, Clara wondered why everything was happening so quickly.

The answer to that question would not be pleasing in the least.

CHAPTER SEVEN

WILLIAM HAD TO admit that the dinner the night before had gone splendidly well. As always, Clara had been entertaining. Once the idea of the proposal had sunk in, she'd been asking questions all evening to both him and his mother.

As he'd expected, his mother had declared her delightful. His father had approved of the match, affirming she'd be a perfect match for his somber personality.

Although Clara's father had been a bit reserved about the proposal, he'd come around during after-dinner drinks. Rightfully so, Albert Humphries was fiercely protective of his daughters and wanted to ensure Clara would be well cared for. He'd seemed mollified when William told him in private, he'd allow Clara to remain in the London townhouse with every expense left to her discretion.

Now in his bedroom, he paced, considering how much longer he'd be forced to remain in the city. After one or two social events where the engagement would be made public and several perfunctory dinners, he hoped to be able to return to Berkhamsted.

If all went well, he'd be home right after the Christmas holiday.

Outside, the moonlight was bright on the newly-fallen

snow, giving it the illusion of being blue. The different tones made for a serene scene. If he were gifted in art, this would definitely be a scene he'd like to capture.

Just a few weeks, perhaps three, and his wish would come true. A solitary life in the country and a wife and children in the city that would make his parents happy were all he wished for.

THE NEXT DAY after breakfast and being asked tons of questions by his mother, William was glad to escape with his hounds. He walked them down the street toward Hyde Park where he'd release them for a bit. The excited dogs tugged on the leashes ensuring they'd keep a fast pace.

Most of the snow had melted and just enough sun peaked through the clouds to make the weather pleasant. There were quite a few people about. On the corner was a man selling roasted chestnuts, his young daughter offering the bundles to passersby.

Not too far ahead was a group of boys playing a game of chase, running in circles and shouting.

It was best to take the dogs away from that area, William decided, as they'd no doubt want to join in the game.

"William," a woman called out. He turned to see her, Rachel Witting, walking toward him, a maid in tow.

Her face was framed with the hood of a fur-lined cape. One would consider Rachel a beauty if not for the harshness of her flattened lips and narrowed eyes. She'd been his lover years back and had not taken his lack of a marriage proposal well. It was one of the many reasons he'd avoided London for the last couple of seasons.

"Rachel." He touched the brim of his hat and attempted

to control the dogs that were not pleased at him standing for so long.

Her narrowed gaze assessed him from head to toe before sliding a glance to the hounds. "Am I to presume you did not receive my message?"

She went straight to the matter at hand as was her custom. William wondered how and why he'd ever ended up in the woman's bed. It had been her who'd contrived the assignations and he the dumb one who'd not seen through her ploy.

"I did and I am flattered that you wish to continue to see me. However, I am not in a position to accept your alluring proposition."

Her eyebrows shot up and disappeared behind the edge of her hood. "Why is that?"

An announcement of the engagement was to be made at a gathering that evening. His mother and Clara's would be most displeased if the news was out before then. However, he saw no other way to get rid of Rachel.

"I am just recently engaged."

The rounding of Rachel's eyes followed the soft gasp. "Is that so? To whom?"

"It will be announced at the Burlingtons' soiree tonight. I cannot possibly divulge any particulars before then. My fiancée and my mother would be most displeased."

Her face became rigid, the features hard until it seemed like a mask. "I will be there and so help you, if you are lying…"

"Don't ever threaten me," William spoke through clenched teeth. "How long until you accept that you and I have no future? I will not marry you ever. I wish for children and so do my parents."

She let out a breath. "You have no idea how powerful I

am. If I wish to ruin your chances at marriage to some young chit, I can do so easily." She snapped her fingers. "Just like that."

"You need to find another man. One that is afraid of your threats. I, for one, find them boring. It doesn't matter what you do. You and I will never be together again."

"We'll see," Rachel snapped and whirled on her heel. The maid gave him an apologetic look before hurrying after her mistress.

It could prove to be a bother if Rachel decided to make some sort of scene at the event that night. As he continued on his walk, William pondered what to do about her threats. Clara was witty and able to defend herself in a war of words. Of that, he had no doubts. However, she was young still and surely not seasoned enough to withstand any kind of attack by a woman like Rachel.

EVENING CAME TOO soon and William found he still had no idea how to deal with the situation. Hopefully, Rachel had just been upset by his announcement and her threats had no substance. If anything came up, he'd have to handle it on the spot.

"There you are, darling," his mother said, entering the room. The deep purple gown suited her perfectly. Although he'd inherited his father's solemn disposition and height, William looked more like his mother.

She rounded him and looked over his attire. "Must you always wear such dark colors? Honestly, William, it's not only a festive season because of the holiday, but you've also just gotten engaged. Perhaps a lighter cravat and not black?"

Black suited him. He didn't have to decide what color

went with what. However, his mother was right. "I only have black."

His mother frowned and William let out a sigh. "I will borrow one of father's then."

When they left the house, two carriages were prepared and waiting. In one, his parents were to head straight to the ball. In the second, he and Alexander would go to the Humphries' home so he and Clara could enter together.

Clara was resplendent in a light blue ball gown. The flush across her cheeks suited her, making her pretty eyes stand out. Her plump lips, which constantly enticed him to want to kiss her, were bright pink.

She, along with Vivian, curtsied as he and Alexander stood by waiting to see who would come with them in the carriage. Penelope, the youngest sister, emerged. Behind her were the Humphries and, lastly, an older woman, who he assumed would be the chaperone.

The woman was introduced as Clara's Aunt Helen. The austere woman barely curtsied, seeming to find fault with both William and Alexander. "I require assistance to climb into your carriage. It seems higher than it needs to be," the woman proclaimed as the coachman hurried to help her.

"Aunt Helen is quite talented," Clara whispered. "She can find fault in everything, no matter how minute. It's astonishing really."

"Noted," William replied, holding out his arm.

Once they were seated, the sisters on either side of Aunt Helen and he and Alexander facing them, the carriage continued its trip to the ball.

EVERY BALLROOM BECAME hot and airless soon after events commenced. This evening, however, the air seemed to have left as soon as Clara and William entered. The conversations in the room dimmed as every guest turned to look when they crossed the threshold into the room. She almost dropped her hand from his arm if not for his firm hand over it.

"Take a deep breath and smile," William said, not looking to her, his face serene.

Clara's breath hitched when she attempted the first time. However, the second try worked.

The steadiness of William's arm and his assuredness helped Clara maintain her composure. Although looks of disbelief made her want to run from the room, she kept a serene smile. When women looked at William with admiration, she had to fight the urge to gloat. It would definitely be unbecoming to stick out her tongue at the jealous ones.

"How delightful that you and your parents came to my small gala," Lady Burlington exclaimed. Her shrewd gaze moved quickly over to Clara. "And you as well, of course, Clara. Why, it's been over a year since I've seen you."

The woman was not particularly nice, which was why Clara and her family rarely attended any event held by the Burlingtons. Given to dramatically long-winded descriptions of her travels, once she began, it was hard to disengage from the one-sided conversations.

Of course, William had no way of knowing. So Clara kept a keen ear to make sure to save them in case Lady Burlington decided to talk of her last trip.

Clara curtsied low. "Lady Burlington, I love your gown. The color is most complementary."

"Thank you, dear." The woman beamed. "I'm sorry, but I can't say the same. I'd have chosen a different color if I were you."

Biting on the inside of her cheek to keep from saying something she'd regret, Clara only nodded. Fortunately, someone else came forward and Lady Burlington excused herself.

"Why are we here?" William groaned. That made Clara chuckle.

"Apparently so that I can be told how horrible my dress is."

His gaze went from her face to her chest then trailed down from there. Heat filled her in a way that she'd never experienced. "I find the gown quite alluring."

Despite knowing he sought to distract her, she blushed at the compliment. When he offered his arm and led her to the dance floor, all was forgotten. For the first time in her life, Clara was the center of attention. The music commenced. While she and William circled, moved apart and came back together along with the other partners, she was aware of every eye on them.

Although he didn't smile, his warm gaze kept her grounded. It was as if she floated just above the floor and could barely keep her eyes from William's face. He, on the other hand, remained composed, turning his attention to whomever he partnered with during the intricate dance.

"A surprising turn of events," Randolph Doolittle commented as they circled. "Rather abrupt engagement," he finished.

Clara gave him as innocent a look as she could muster. "It seems some men do not dawdle for years before making a declaration."

The glare was cut short when Randolph was forced to turn away and join again with his partner.

The dance ended and William escorted Clara to a side area. "I'll get you something to drink."

Moments later, a couple came over to introduce themselves to William. The man pulled him aside while the woman attempted at conversation with Clara. The awkward woman's eyes rounded when another woman, one Clara had never met, approached.

Despite a bit too much rouge on her cheeks and a bit too strong a perfume, the woman seemed to attract the attention of the men who surrounded them.

The woman who'd been speaking to Clara immediately excused herself and hurried away.

"I heard the news of your engagement to Viscount Torrington," the woman who'd approached said. "Congratulations are in order."

There was something about this woman Clara didn't like, but manners took over. "You have me at a disadvantage. I don't know who you are."

"I am Rachel Witting, your soon-to-be husband's lover."

Clara blinked, not sure she'd heard the woman correctly. "I see."

The woman's eyes hardened at her lack of expression. "It's best you hear it from me. At least that is what William and I decided earlier today when we spoke."

"What am I supposed to say to that?" Clara maintained a neutral expression although her heart threatened to explode from her chest. William had his back turned and continued in conversation with the man who'd approached. They'd been joined by yet another.

"It's natural, of course," the woman continued. "Men need a woman with experience, especially when married to a young innocent such as you. There is no need to fret."

At the last comment, Clara lost her temper. Seeming to sense her anger, William turned. His eyes flickered to the woman, Rachel, and rounded, but only for a fleeting second.

She didn't need him to approach and save her. Clara was perfectly able to defend herself from the horrid woman. Mustering all her strength, Clara smiled at the woman. Although she kept her attention on Rachel's face, she was dimly aware William was nearing.

"I'm not sure why he would tell you I am innocent and inexperienced. Perhaps, he didn't wish to hurt your feelings being that you're obviously quite older than me. I'd say even a great deal older than William. Or perhaps, it could be your overabundance of '*experience*' has aged you."

The woman swallowed and was about to say something when William arrived. He stood at Clara's right and took her elbow. "We must speak about your choice in who you speak to in public, darling." He whisked her away before Clara could object.

"I was about to say something clever and you stole the opportunity from me," she protested.

"What did she tell you?" Eyebrows furrowed, he studied her. "Tell me."

"No, I will not." Clara jutted her chin out. If he was, indeed, an adulterer and planned to keep a mistress, there was little she could do. However, she needed to find out more about the woman. Perhaps, others knew of any assignation between William and the horrid, face-painted woman.

"There's my sister. I must speak to her."

Indeed, across the salon were Vivian and Mr. Yarnsby. When her sister snatched her dance card from the man and stormed away, Clara could not believe her eyes.

Her normally gentle sister rarely lost her temper. "Will

you excuse me?" she said to William. He nodded, his expression stormy at her lack of acquiescence.

Vivian stood just outside the salon doors. Her serene expression almost caused Clara to miss the hard set of her mouth and slight lift of her chin.

"What happened? Did Mr. Yarnsby insult you?" Clara took her sister's hands.

"Mr. Yarnsby is dimwitted."

It took all her willpower not to laugh. "What did he do?"

"Nothing. He never does anything."

"Oh?"

Vivian let out a long sigh. "Never mind. Let's go back inside. I must find Glenda. I hear she may be back from India and here tonight. You and I should arrange an invitation to have tea with her."

Unbeknownst to their mother, the sisters enjoyed tea with their dear friend. Although just a couple years older than them, Glenda Grant was well traveled and experienced in more ways than one would expect. The information they'd gleaned over the last couple of years had drawn them to return often.

When Glenda announced a trip to India with her husband, Clara had been disappointed. It seemed now was the perfect timing for her friend's return.

"We must find her. I have questions." Clara took her sister's hand, but didn't move. William and Mr. Yarnsby stood just inside. "Let's go back through the other door."

Once inside, the distraction of the music and dancing helped Clara calm down. However, as the minutes ticked by, it became obvious William had either left or was in the gentlemen's area.

Finally, after an hour, Clara was incensed. It was their first appearance as an engaged couple and he was nowhere to be found.

"Walk about the room with me," she prodded Penelope who'd just returned from dancing, her cheeks flushed from the heat. "I haven't seen William anywhere."

While Penelope chatted about the men she'd danced with, obviously unaware of Clara's dark mood, they walked every inch of the ballroom and even down the hallway to peer into the library where men lounged smoking cigars.

William had left. It was then it occurred to Clara that the woman, Rachel, had disappeared as well.

THE RIDE BACK home was done mostly in silence. Mr. Yarnsby accompanied them back. Although he made excuses for William's absence, it was obvious the man had no idea where his friend had gone.

CHAPTER EIGHT

"WHAT THE HELL do you think you're doing?"
William struggled to sit up, but he'd been bound
with ropes around his torso and legs. "If it's money you want,
you may as well forget about it. I've instructed my family not
to ever pay a dime."

The smell of rotten fish made him struggle not to gag. It
wouldn't do to throw up and then lay in it. Although there
was shuffling of feet, he couldn't turn to see who the people
were.

"We're just keepin' you for a bit," a man said, his scratchy
voice telling of many years of bad living. "Already been paid
for it, too." There were chuckles combined with coughing.

"Who hired you?"

Footsteps retreated then the unmistakable sound of a door
closing.

"Let me out now!" William called. But he was drowned
out by the sounds of fishermen's calls outside.

A few moments later, one of the men returned and
wrapped a dirty cloth around his mouth. "That should keep
you silent for a bit." He laughed and walked out.

WHAT SEEMED LIKE an eternity later, his captors finally returned. By then, it was dim outside. He guessed it to be early morning. They untied his now numb arms and legs.

The men then left, mumbling about finding something to eat.

For a long while, he was unable to stand. So, he sat on the ground and waited for feeling to come into his arms and legs. He had no idea who would have wanted to hold him captive for a day and not demand anything in return.

No doubt, his parents and Alexander assumed he'd gotten an invitation from a woman and had left the party.

Hopefully, they knew him well enough to realize he'd never do it without telling someone, or at least escorting Clara home.

Clara. He wondered how she'd reacted to his absence. No doubt, she was angry with him.

Finally able to stand, he walked out onto the docks. A few men sat about drinking and chatting. They watched him with curiosity, but none made any comment or spoke to him. Obviously his disheveled appearance wasn't an oddity. No doubt, this was a location to bring someone kidnapped.

"Unbelievable," William muttered.

"WHERE HAVE YOU been?" His mother met him at the door, brows furrowed. "Your father and Alex have been out looking for you since last night."

She sniffed at him. "Goodness, Son, you smell horrible."

"I was kidnapped," Alexander snapped. "A pair of idiots hit me on the head, took me to the docks and bound me. Then, without explanation, they released me just now."

His mother's eyes widened and she placed a hand across her chest. "Oh, my. Are you injured?" She reached for his face. "Charles, call a doctor immediately."

Face etched with concern, Charles hurried to them. "Yes, My Lady." He looked to William. "Come this way, My Lord. I'll see about cleaning you up and promptly throwing out those clothes."

Later that day, he'd been examined to exhaustion, thoroughly questioned by the police and given several glasses of brandy. His mother would not allow him to do much more than recline as she constantly hovered over him.

Alexander looked on. "Have you decided whether or not to send word to Clara? She was most put out last night."

"That makes two of us," William replied. "I am not sure what to do about all of this. It makes no sense and, honestly, I fear looking like a fool."

His friend nodded in understanding. "Perhaps sending a note of apology or, better yet, paying a visit would be advisable."

THE NEXT DAY, he felt better although he'd woken with a start not quite sure of where he was.

On the way to visit Clara, he decided it was best to invite her for a ride in the park and then he'd retreat to Berkhamsted for a couple of weeks. Whoever was out to harm him would have a hard time finding him there. It made no sense what the objective of his abduction was. However, he didn't want to take a chance that it would affect Clara.

A solemn butler ushered him to the parlor. He didn't have to wait long before Clara appeared. "William." She gave a slight curtsy. "Good morning."

Her formality did not surprise him. Obviously, she was quite angry with him. "Clara. I owe you an apology for my disappearance last evening."

Instead of a reply, her left eyebrow rose and she looked at him in question. "I can't wait to hear what you have to say, My Lord."

She'd never addressed him formally, even upon learning of his title. William had to clear his throat. How was it possible this young woman unsettled him so? "You see, I became ill and was forced to leave immediately."

"Is that so?" She studied him for a moment. "You seem to have recovered well."

"Yes…well, I feel much better…" He wasn't sure what else to say. On the way there, he'd prepared with the name of the doctor who'd come to his home. However, now it seemed that the more he said the less she'd believe him.

"I came to invite you out for a drive. It's a nice day out."

"I would love to, however, my sister, Vivian, and I have an engagement this afternoon." She stood as if dismissing him.

"Clara." He approached her, not liking that she stiffened at his proximity. "I am truly sorry for leaving last night. It was completely out of my control."

Although she remained angry, her eyes moved down to his mouth. Clara was attracted to him and desired his touch. Just as much as he desired her.

Although, William conceded, he wanted much more than a kiss from his fetching fiancée.

"Allow me to kiss you, Clara." He approached, not waiting for her to reply and pulled her against him. Although she remained still, Clara did not protest.

When he leaned in to kiss her, her lips parted in expectation. It was all the invitation he needed. At the moment,

William wanted to feel alive, to taste her and take what was offered.

Their mouths met, and William could not help letting out a sigh at the taste of her. He was not gentle. He needed to show her how much he desired her. The kiss deepened. She released a light moan when he slipped his hand down her bodice to cup her left breast. She was well endowed, her soft flesh overfilling his palm.

Clara lifted up to her toes and he covered her mouth once again to muffle her soft moan when he ran the pad of his thumb over the tight bud of her nipple.

Her fingers clutched at his lapels when he thrust his tongue into her mouth as he continued to stroke her breast.

It was more than he could take and unfortunately William became arouse and hard. Releasing her breast and breaking the kiss, William let out a long breath. "I cannot wait to marry you."

"I am not sure what to say right now. I am still angry about last night," she replied with a lift of her pert nose. Her chest heaved with each breath.

He smiled at her and pressed a kiss the tip. "I understand. However, I cannot begin to explain my absence. I do assure you it was not something I planned, nor desired."

Her beautiful eyes narrowed. "I'd prefer if you'd not insult me by making up excuses. It's obvious that regardless of the fact there is a physical attraction between us, our engagement is nothing more than a social obligation."

"It is more than that," he snapped, not sure what, exactly, he meant by it. Hopefully, she'd not ask.

Clara huffed and rolled her eyes. "You should go. I have things to do."

"As you wish. However, I will tell you this. I do not make

it a habit to shirk from what is expected of me."

Her gaze moved past him to the far wall and William wanted to take her by the shoulders and shake her.

"I suppose I shouldn't take more of your precious time. I will take my leave. I am going to Berkhamsted for a few days to see about a matter that needs my immediate attention. Upon my return, I will come to see you promptly."

"A few days?" Clara's eyes widened. "What about our social obligations. We've accepted invitations to at least three upcoming events."

"Please ensure to go. Enjoy yourself."

"Ugh." Clara set her jaw. "I will not make excuses for you."

"What is the matter? I can hear you down the hall." Her mother entered and looked to William and then to Clara. "Already having a row?"

Clara huffed. "He is leaving. Returning to Berkhamsted for a few days. Despite our social obligations."

The matriarch met his gaze. "I do find that rather alarming."

"I do apologize. I promise to be swift about returning."

His fiancée stalked away from him. "Perhaps this engagement is a bad idea. I think you proposed rashly and are now changing your mind."

"We both know I have not changed my mind about you at all." He met her gaze and then lowered his eyes to her breasts.

She colored and looked away.

"Yes...I see," her mother stuttered obviously having guessed what had transpired between them. "My Lord, I suggest you make haste and return as soon as possible. Tongues will wag otherwise."

"I'm sure with a certain two people missing at the same time last night, the tongues have already been loosed," Clara said. When she looked down and clutched her hands together, it was obvious how much the incident had hurt her.

"Who else was gone?"

She didn't reply. Instead, she turned her attention to the doorway. "Have a pleasant trip, My Lord."

RIDING BACK TO the townhouse, William was torn about whether he should leave or not. He'd never been a coward to run from a threat. Although the incident had been disturbing, he'd not been hurt or worse.

London was oppressive, he couldn't think clearly. Yes, perhaps, his fogged brain had something to do with the slip of a girl he was engaged to. However, the fact he was threatened was not something to take lightly given the fact he'd soon be responsible for not only his welfare, but Clara's as well.

BACK AT THE townhouse, William sought out his cousin.

"So you have no idea who would do this?" Alexander asked.

"No. However, Clara alluded to someone else leaving the party at the same time. Any idea who that that could be?"

His friend shrugged. "There were many in attendance. Who were you speaking to last?"

"A couple who had been to Berkhamsted and contemplated purchasing an estate there and Clara. Of course the hosts." William stopped and sat up.

"Clara was speaking to Rachel Witting at one point. I

drew her away, hopefully before the woman said too much."

"Do you think she would do something like this?"

William had no idea what Rachel was capable of doing. However, she had been put out with him when he'd turned down her offer of continuing their assignation.

"A woman scorned is quite dangerous," Alexander quipped. "Perhaps you should have a word with her."

WILLIAM DISMOUNTED AND tethered his horse. It had been folly to ride on that dreary day. The light drizzle had permeated through his thick coat and, although he wasn't wet, the dampness of the clothes made him shiver.

Too restless and annoyed to wait for a carriage to be prepared, he'd sought his favorite horse, Zeus. The huge beast was always at the ready to be released from the stables. Like him, the horse was not keen on remaining in the city.

Making quick work of the steps up to the front door of the townhouse, William knocked and waited for the butler to open the panel. An austere man with a face that drooped on the left side stood in the doorway, his eyes flickering with recognition.

"My Lord, please come in. It's quite cold outside." He looked past him to Zeus, who pranced in place. "Should I have a footman see about your steed, My Lord?"

"No, thank you. I won't be long."

"Very well, I will announce your presence to Mrs. Witting."

William almost groaned out loud as the man took one step and then another, seeming to hesitate between each. The butler should have retired years ago; even then he was as slow as a turtle.

"This way, My Lord," the butler said when he finally returned.

If not for his foul mood, he would have laughed at having to remain behind the man to enter Rachel's parlor.

Rachel looked up as if in surprise. She lifted an eyebrow. "What do I owe this visit to? Did you change your mind and expect me to fall backward and accept your body?"

"Not in the least," William replied and remained standing. Even if the woman had invited him to sit, he would have declined.

She lifted a cup of what he presumed was tea to her lips, but didn't sip. "Now you have piqued my curiosity."

As always, Rachel was overly made up. For the time of day, the rouge and kohl lining her eyes made her appear harsh. She could be described as attractive. However, since his return, he found she'd aged and there was something different about her. A cloud seemed to hover over her.

"I want to understand the reason behind the men attacking my person," he said without preamble.

Rachel didn't pretend not to understand. Instead, her gaze raked over him. "I don't see any kind of injury." She focused on a light bruise on his jaw. "The purpling on your jaw doesn't mar that pretty face much."

"Answer my question."

He almost took a step back when she dropped the teacup to the floor and stood. "I don't owe you any kind of explanation, Viscount Torrington. As a matter of fact, I'm tired of the expectations of entitled men like you." Her eyes narrowed until they were almost slits.

"Year after year, I have laid on my back for you and others only to be treated as a stranger in public. Every single one of you has discarded me once you grew tired or bored."

Not about to allow her to pile her bitterness on him, William let out a huff. "We had an agreement from the very beginning. If I remember correctly, it was you who first mentioned a desire for a discreet arrangement with no attachments or expectations."

Her gaze shifted, but she snarled after a moment. "Of course. Otherwise, you would have dashed from me. It was what you expected."

The accusations made little sense. He studied her and realized something was wrong. Her eyes were unfocused and her cheekbones more pronounced. Her coloring was off as well.

Rachel Witting was very ill. If he were to guess, she was not long for this world. Why would she wish to cause harm and not enjoy what time she had left?

"I won't remain here and argue with you. If I hurt you in any way, I offer my apologies. However, as you may remember, I live away from London and did not wish to return to the city. I informed you of this so that you'd understand my absence."

Her shoulders rounded as she lowered back to sit. "I don't care for apologies. What I do care about is that if I can ruin just one of your lives, it will be a little bit of fairness." She looked to the door. "You shouldn't have come to annoy me."

The chuckle that came next made William's hair stand on end. It was so filled with hatred. Rachel's lips curved. "I doubt that idiotic, naïve girl, Clara, will want to marry you after this. After all, she comes from a perfect home, with perfect parents. Why would she want to marry someone as imperfect as you?"

As if on cue, there was a knock at the front door. Moments later, the butler slogged past. Without announcement, Lady Harriet Montclair, the most prolific gossip of London society strolled in.

CHAPTER NINE

"I AM NOT sure what to think," her mother whispered to Lady Barrow. The breathlessness of it made Clara, who was walking past the parlor, hesitate.

There was a light sound of a teacup on a plate. "It's the talk of the town. How the viscount abandoned Clara and then was found by none other than Lady Montclair in that woman's home."

They spoke of William. Had he gone to see Rachel Witting after they'd spoken? Her heart hammered as she moved closer to the doorway, not caring if the women inside saw her or not.

Her mother blew out a breath. "There has to be a plausible explanation. Whatever should we do?"

"We should cancel the engagement," Clara said from the doorway. "This is unacceptable. I won't marry him. He's a scoundrel."

Her mother stood and drew her to sit. Lady Borrow gave Clara an understanding smile. The warmth in the woman's eyes almost brought Clara to cry. "Don't be brash, dear. It could all be a horrible misunderstanding. Tell us, did he explain why he left the party?"

Clara nodded. "Yes, he said it was because he became ill.

He also said a doctor had been called."

The entire situation was mortifying. And now that London society knew about the affair, it would be impossible to show her face in public. The looks of pity and curiosity would be her undoing. No matter how independent she considered herself, this type of experience would be hard to withstand.

"I will not attend the dinner tonight, Mother." Clara stood and left the room, needing the privacy of her bedroom.

THE SILENCE OF the empty house made Clara restless. She'd feigned a headache so as not to attend the evening's event. Although her mother had understood, immediately agreeing she should remain home, her sisters had been very disappointed.

Her sour mood would have dampened any enjoyment by her sisters. Now as she paced the empty bedroom, her mind constantly went from the kiss the night before to the fact that William had gone to Rachel Witting's home. She wondered if he went to inform her he was leaving town or to invite her to go with him. It could be that they were making plans for a tryst when Lady Montclair had discovered them.

Was it possible he and Rachel were going to his country estate together? Why had William proposed to her if he was enamored with another woman? Of course, it could be that the woman was older than William and could not produce an heir.

She, on the other hand, was younger and would be able to bear children.

Then there was the possibility that because of Rachel's reputation for taking lovers, his family would never accept the woman.

Tea earlier that day with Glenda had been most enlightening. She'd divulged that Rachel Witting was not liked at all by the women of their social circles. The widow had taken quite a few lovers, most of them married.

The only reason Rachel was invited to social events was to add fodder for gossip and make the gatherings more interesting.

Clara almost felt sorry for the woman. Why would anyone subject themselves to such occurrences? It made little sense.

Abruptly, Clara decided that, perhaps, it was silly to not take action.

Obviously, William had given little thought to her when deciding to leave and go to the country.

Rushing from the room, she went upstairs to her bedroom.

ONCE HER CARRIAGE arrived at the gathering just a few blocks away, Clara became nervous and, instead, directed the driver to take her to the Torrington townhouse.

Then upon arriving there, once again, she wondered at the folly of her ways.

She waited in the quiet evening bundled in her cloak until a butler hurried over to the carriage and informed her Lady Theresa was excited at the prospect of spending time with her. Her hands trembled and her legs threatened to give out from under her as she descended from the carriage and walked to the entrance. This was most forward of her, to arrive without warning.

Thankfully, the chill of the air cooled down her overly-heated face. Hopefully, any reddening would be blamed on the weather.

William's mother greeted her at the doorway with a wide smile. Hands extended, she took Clara's in her own and guided her inside. "I am delighted that you are here."

"I beg your pardon at coming without sending more notice. I find myself a bit confused and not sure who to speak to."

"Minerva, see that tea and biscuits are brought. Thank you, dear." The maid who'd been standing at the doorway left and after Clara's cloak was done away with, both women sat.

"It has been an upsetting couple of days. I don't blame you for being confused. I am not sure what William told you. I don't agree with his decision to return to Berkhamsted. I informed him it was horrible timing and a bad idea. Now, he is brooding about it."

Clara's stomach pitched. If William were there, what would his reaction be? "He hasn't left then?"

"Not as yet. He and Alexander had business with an actuary today. After, they were to see a tailor who is measuring William for his wedding attire."

Speechless, she realized she'd not thought about what he'd be wearing. They'd not even set a date for that matter. "We haven't set a date."

"Yes, I know. Your mother plans for us to have tea the day after tomorrow to discuss it, with you present, of course." Theresa looked to the doorway. "Hopefully, William will have decided to remain in the city."

"Was he truly ill?" Clara wasn't about to mince words. "He told me the doctor had been here to see him."

"A doctor was summoned." Theresa's words were stilted. "Although we were told he was fine, I insisted he rest and remain abed for the rest of the day and night."

"I see." Clara felt bad at not believing him. "Wait, you said day and night. Where was he the night before?"

"Oh, look, here is Minerva with the tea now," Theresa exclaimed much too brightly. "You'll love the biscuits. They are delightful."

When tea was served, Clara noticed two large dogs by the hearth. They were sleeping soundly, seeming to being accustomed to people coming and going.

"Are those William's dogs?"

Theresa smiled indulgently in the direction of the slumbering beasts. "Yes. The reddish one is Ellington and the darker one is Farnsworth. He named them after his tutors growing up."

"They seem content."

"Yes, they are exhausted. Charles, our butler, took them for a long walk earlier and they've just been fed. Both are horribly pampered."

Clara lifted the teacup to her lips. She had so many questions, but wasn't sure how to proceed exactly.

"Now, about William. Darling, you have nothing to worry about. He is quite enchanted by you. I know my son can tend to be headstrong. He has been so since he was a boy. However, I know him well enough to tell you he will marry you and be a wonderful husband."

"That is not what I have doubts about. I do believe he finds me attractive and that he will fulfill his obligation." Clara hesitated, unsure of her words. "It's just that I find it alarming that he left me alone at the gathering the other night and then plans to leave in the middle of our first social obligations." She purposely left out the information about the rumors flying around. It would, no doubt, hurt the kind woman and it would be best if she heard it from someone else.

Theresa straightened. "I will have a word with my husband and ask that someone go to Berkhamsted to see about whatever needs William's attention so suddenly. Perhaps Alexander can go in his stead."

"I am not sure I should interfere in this," Clara replied, wondering what it mattered now that the gossips would be chomping at the bit to see them together.

"Interfere you must. Not just about this matter, but also about his plans for you to remain in London after the marriage."

Seeming to realize what she'd said, Theresa covered her mouth with one hand. "Oh, goodness. I can't seem to keep from saying the wrong things."

"What do you mean, I will remain in London?"

Her future mother-in-law's shoulders fell. "I am sure he planned to tell you. He told your father. I suppose it's best I do. Once you are married, William plans to return to Berkhamsted alone and visit London regularly. My son is convinced a woman from London would die of boredom in the country."

She'd have a chat with her father immediately.

"My place is to be with my husband. I don't understand." Clara put her cup down because her hands shook so hard that she feared dropping it. "Why plan to marry if he doesn't want to live with me? What about children?"

"Oh, there is that. He has assured us that he would be sure you become with child..."

"And be left alone throughout my pregnancy and to raise said child as well, I presume."

Theresa attempted to smile and failed. "I've said too much. I am not sure his plans remain the same actually."

"No," Clara interjected. "I think they absolutely do. Thank you for telling me all of this. It gives me more time to grow accustomed to the idea of what to expect." To her horror, a tear trickled down her cheek. It was all too much to take in at once.

"Oh, please don't cry. We will figure something out. I promise." Theresa pulled a handkerchief from her sleeve and held it out to Clara.

"Good evening," William said from the door. When he noticed Clara wiping her eyes, his gaze flew back and forth between her and his mother.

He approached slowly, Alexander Yarnsby just behind him. "Did something happen?"

Clara turned away, not wanting to face him just yet. No matter how angry and hurt she was, her traitorous body instantly reacted to his presence. Butterflies took flight in her stomach and her chest constricted at the sound of his voice.

Theresa interjected, "There is nothing wrong, Son. It is just that Clara and I were discussing the wedding and she became emotional."

He would have probably believed his mother if Clara could've kept from glaring at him.

William's eyebrows rose and he exchanged looks with Alexander who backed out of the room.

"What can I do to help?" he asked. Clara held back the urge to tell him to leave and never come back.

Fortunately, her future mother-in-law decided it was a good time for them to talk alone. "I think I'll check to see if Minerva has more of these delicious biscuits."

Once the woman left, Clara took a long breath and did her best to compose herself.

"Perhaps it is best if we cancel the engagement. You can

go back to your solitary life in the country and I can find a husband that does not require a mistress," Clara stated. Her sharp tone was unrestrained as she remained firmly annoyed.

There was a noticeable tick in William's jaw as he fought to maintain control. Clara was delighted to know she'd angered him. It was about time. It was not just her who'd lost reign of her emotions.

"You know good and well, anything of that nature would ruin you and your sister's chances for a good match. We will marry and I am sure we can come to an agreeable arrangement as to where we will live."

"We will either live here in London or in Berkhamsted…together. I refused to be tied down diapering and wiping the noses of your bothersome children while you play bachelor."

"What makes you think our children will be troublesome? Are you unsure of your parenting abilities?"

"How can you ask that? If they are anything like you, I am sure they will be headstrong and annoying."

He stood and stalked to the fireplace. "This is not the conversation we should be having just weeks before marrying."

"Oh, pray tell me, My Lord, do we have a date? Do you plan to inform me or should I ask Rachel Witting, who no doubt is more informed."

William's hands curled into fists and he let out a long breath. His gray eyes were dark with anger and, for an instant, Clara wondered if she'd gone too far.

"Clara," he started. "I have nothing to do with Rachel Witting, not any longer. I did two years ago. It was a mistake. She, however, is not above causing problems."

Clara stood. "Is she the reason you plan to leave and go to

Berkhamsted? Tell me why were you with her yesterday? Or do you plan to tell me it didn't happen?"

For a moment, he paused and frowned. "I am not having an affair."

He had not answered her question. Not really. Clara stood.

"I'm going home. It's quite late." Clara was astounded by how fast he was in front of her blocking any way to escape the room.

"I don't wish you to leave and still remain angry with me." The deepness of his voice seemed to reach out and caress her. Clara hated that no matter how annoyed she was, he still managed to affect her so.

She hitched her chin up. Somehow, she'd muddle through and put off the wedding long enough for her sisters to find husbands.

"Our next social engagement is not until four days from now. Perhaps, we need the time apart to calm down. I find that I am too angry with you at this moment to be reasonable."

Once again, the muscle on his jaw bunched and released. "I will go to Berkhamsted then and return in time. I need time away to consider how to keep you safe from anything Mrs. Witting could have planned."

It was hard to keep from shoving past him. "She is but a widow searching for a lover. I'm sure I am the least of her concerns."

CHAPTER TEN

"I AM NOT sure I agree that you should leave town so unexpectedly, Clara," her mother said as she frowned over breakfast the next day. "Although I'm sure my sister will be glad for the visit."

Clara waited without speaking. Molly, her personal maid, was already preparing for the trip. She'd dispatched the girl to see about the carriage and ensure they had what they needed for the overnight trip.

"It's only for two days. I want to visit and spend the night with Aunt Bettina and then return. I desperately need the change of scenery to clear my head."

Her father finally deemed it important enough to peer at her from over the papers he read. "Make sure you bring back some of her shortbread."

"Oh, Albert, do you honestly think there will be time for them to make shortbread?" her mother replied, chuckling. "Although I don't doubt my sister will make it. She adores you."

Just over an hour later, Clara and Molly were ensconced in the carriage, the horses making quick work of taking them away from London.

"I am so glad you and the new coachman, Jeffrey, have

become fast friends. It allows us to go where we wish with no questions. He doesn't know enough to ask," Clara said and smiled when Molly blushed.

"I am not sure if I'd exactly call us fast friends, Miss Clara. But he did agree to take us to Berkhamsted straightaway."

Clara peered out the window. "Thankfully, it's but an hour away from where Aunt Bettina lives. We can see about Lord Torrington and then be on our way."

There was a bit of silence as Clara nibbled on her bottom lip. "Where were my sisters off to? It proved quite timely that they'd gone with the other carriage. However, I find it off-putting that I wasn't involved in whatever plot Penelope has come up with."

"I believe it has to do with Mr. Yarnsby, Miss. Miss Vivian is not at all happy with the way he is running off suitors with his glares and such."

At recalling the man's visit the night before, Clara smiled. "He is most extraordinary. The way he keeps his distance and yet seems to surround Vivian at all times. And yet, he refuses to court her. I find it very odd."

Molly shrugged as she was not in a position, nor would it be proper for her to give her opinion on someone like Mr. Yarnsby.

WHEN THEY ARRIVED just outside Lark's Song, William's country estate, Clara instructed Jeffrey to slow and come to a stop just outside the gates.

The young man climbed down from his perch and rounded the carriage, giving her a quizzical look. However, he did not question her instructions and, within moments, took the carriage to a nearby cusp of trees to wait for her and Molly to return.

On the ride to Berkhamsted, she'd donned a sturdy, gray gown and serviceable boots that would withstand a trek through muddy ground and foliage.

"We'll make quick work of arriving from the side of the house," Clara explained to her maid. Already, her pulse was racing at the thought of what lay ahead.

"Remain low to the ground and we must stay along the walls," she instructed her maid.

"Yes, Miss Clara," Molly said, her face bright with excitement. "Shouldn't you cover your hair?"

"Oh, yes, thank you, Molly. I almost forgot." She yanked a sleeping cap from her pocket and quickly shoved her hair into it.

It wasn't a long walk, so they had to take care to keep hidden. Clara and Molly crept along slowly until reaching the house.

The only plan she had was to peer through the windows and see if Rachel Witting was about. If the hateful woman was there, Clara would then retreat back to the carriage and once back in London she'd do her best to avoid social obligations and William Torrington. There had to be a way to do it without harming her sisters.

They finally arrived at a large set of windows. Unfortunately, they were much too high to look into. Clara scowled. She'd not considered that the bottom of the windows would be above their heads.

"Crumpets, what can we do now?" she whispered to Molly. "We need something to stand on."

Molly looked around. "I'll go around to the front and see if the windows there are lower."

Before she could take a step, Clara grabbed her hand and yanked her backward. "No. Someone, a servant or William, could spy you."

Her remark was silly, of course, since someone could very well see them no matter where they peered in.

"Look," Molly exclaimed much too loudly, pointing at a pile of firewood. "That's right under a window."

Clara could barely keep from racing to the woodpile. However, she remembered it was best to be quiet and keep from alerting anyone of their presence.

"I'll go first, Miss. It would be best for me to confirm that it's steady. I'd hate for you to be injured or worse." Molly gave her a once over as if ensuring Clara was up for the task.

"Worse?"

Once again, Molly shrugged. "You could break something, be startled by a spider or such."

"It's winter. There are no creatures about." However, Clara couldn't keep from studying the logs.

Once Molly was steady on her feet at the top of the pile and was bent over so not to be seen from the inside, Clara followed suit.

Ever so slowly, she then lifted up to her toes and peered through the window. "Oh, goodness. There is no one in this room but the dogs." It was a large parlor with a stately fireplace that housed a flickering fire. Clara shivered, as the cold wind seemed to seep through her cloak. "I wonder where he is."

Just then, a grumble of voices and movement caught her attention. It was a woman and a man who spoke in quiet tones. Clara ducked.

Her heartbeat quickened at recognizing William's tone. Whoever the woman was, she spoke too softly for Clara to recognize the voice. Her heart plummeted. He was there with Rachel Witting.

"I can't look," she whispered and let out a sigh. "You do it. I want to know who he's talking to."

Eyes round, Molly nodded. "Very well, Miss. Here, let me move closer." The maid inched around Clara until she stood against the house's wall. Then, ever so slowly, she inched up to spy inside.

"Oh, no!" Molly ducked, her face pale. "He saw me."

Barks sounded.

"Oh, goodness." Clara took Molly's arm. "Are you sure?"

Molly nodded emphatically. "He's coming to the window." The maid tried to scramble around her, effectively causing Clara to lose her balance.

Clara tumbled off the woodpile, her head hitting a log with a hard thud. If that weren't bad enough, Molly then finally lost her battle to remain upright and rolled off the woodpile to land atop her. That knocked the breath from her and ruined any chance they had to run away before someone caught them.

Barks sounded closer just as Clara blacked out.

A SOFT RASPING sound woke Clara. She pried her eyes open just a bit to see that the sun had fallen.

Oh, no. She kept her eyes lowered as she tried to look about without turning her head. To her right, there was a large hand on the bed. It held her hand. Further to the right was a long, outstretched leg that was connected to a man's hip. She further noticed a flat stomach and wide chest.

Again the same rasping noise, a snore of sorts sounded. Clara opened her eyes fully to see William fast asleep in a chair, his head at what looked to be an uncomfortable angle. He held her hand in his lax one.

She'd made a colossal fool of herself. And, now, here she was, practically in bed with her betrothed. Her cheeks burned with mortification realizing she no longer wore her clothes.

Where in the blazes was Molly?

Regardless of how absolutely adorable William looked at the moment, he was a rake and a scoundrel. How unfortunate that while she was out from bumping her throbbing head, he'd had a chance to dispatch his mistress and probably Molly and the coachman...Jasper? Jeffrey?

Oh, goodness, did she now suffer from memory loss?

"Are you gasping because you're in pain?" William's sleepy voice made her start.

He slid his hand from hers and peered down at her. "There's a very large bump on the back of your head. We tried our best to bring you to. But when you did come around, you argued and fussed. So after several brave tries by Molly and my staff, everyone surrendered to your temper and allowed you to sleep."

"I don't have a temper." Clara frowned. The back of her head was throbbing. Her temples were joining the celebration with pulses of their own.

William stood. "I'll fetch Molly and ask for something to be brought for your headache. You're probably in need of some privacy."

Why did he act so thoughtful? Then again, rakes were good at making a woman feel special.

"I would like to see Molly. You don't have to do anything for me. Once I dress, I will be on my way. She'll see about the carriage being readied."

His lips twitched. "I feel the need to inform you that it is quite late, perhaps ten at night. Secondly, your coachman was dispatched to London for a doctor."

Clara sat straight up. Her head immediately protested and she ignored it. "No."

The door opened and Molly came straight to her, tears trailing down her cheeks. "Miss Clara, thank God. I was so very worried. How do you feel?"

Annoyed at the girl for allowing the coachman to leave without them, she waved the maid's fears away. "Molly, where exactly is Jeffrey going?"

Molly looked to William and then let out a sniff. "I instructed him to fetch Dr. Appleby."

Dr. Appleby was a large, orange tabby cat they'd both played with when they were children. Although it would distract Jeffrey for a bit, the young man would no doubt go to her family to find out where to find the make-believe doctor.

"I also told him to make haste and ensure that he is not seen by any Humphries."

"You're a dear," Clara said. "However, I don't require a doctor. I must go to Aunt Bettina's house."

William had remained next to the fireplace, despite having said he'd give her privacy. He crossed his arms. "I don't believe you are in any shape to go anywhere. You've also twisted your ankle."

The injury that had been absent came to life with gusto when she wiggled her left foot.

"Ouch!" Clara cried out. "Crumpets and ash!" She fell backward into the pillow and closed her eyes. This was certainly not how things were supposed to be. Her plan had gone horribly wrong.

Nothing had gone as she'd hoped. Her main wish had been for Vivian to marry a wonderful man. She'd dreamed of attending her beautiful sister's wedding and smiling so broadly her cheeks would hurt. This was not supposed to be her life, one awful event right after another.

"I want to go home." She crossed her arms and pushed her head back onto the pillow. "And I don't wish to marry you."

"I do believe our patient is having a temper tantrum again, Molly. Should we give her more laudanum?"

Clara opened her eyes and glared at William. When she looked to her maid, the young woman tried valiantly not to smile. "Once the sun rises, we can be on our way, Miss Clara. I'm sure His Lordship won't mind allowing us to borrow a horse."

"And how will you return said horse?" William's tone was dry. "I don't think he will return of his own volition."

Molly paled.

"Don't be cruel. She was only trying to help," Clara snapped. "Very well. We will await Jeffrey and then once the doctor proclaims me able to travel, we will leave. It shouldn't be longer than mid-afternoon tomorrow."

"It's a three or four hour ride. I doubt Jeffrey will have time to arrive, get rested, replace the horse, find the doctor, convince said doctor to return with him and then arrive by that time."

Clara looked to Molly. "Did you tell Jeffrey where to find Dr. Appleby?"

Her maid once again slid a look to William and nodded. "Yes, of course. I said Dr. Appleby's shop is next to the small coffee shop on Tater's Street. In the alleyway."

Her maid had sent for Jules. William would probably recognize him. Goodness, things were getting worse and worse.

CHAPTER ELEVEN

C LARA WOKE THE next morning ravenous. She could hardly believe how well she'd rested, once getting over the shock of what could happen.

Thankfully, she'd gleaned from Molly that the carriage and one horse remained, which meant they could steal away at a moment's notice. Of course, there was the slight complication of not knowing how to hitch a horse to the wagon. Molly claimed to have observed it done several times. However, she wasn't quite sure what went where.

No matter. Once Jules arrived and pretended to be a doctor, they'd be on their way to her Aunt Bettina's. Then, once she was back in London, she'd explain to her mother that she'd decided to remain an additional day with her aunt.

Unless they talked soon, the sisters would, no doubt, not discuss timetables and such.

Her stomach grumbled just as William entered. Dressed casually, opting not to wear either a cravat or coat, he seemed quite at ease. His thick shirt no doubt kept him warm enough as did the fire in the hearth.

His gaze moved to her. There was something in the way he looked at her, as if gauging what to do about her.

"I've come to fetch you for breakfast. Your maid is sound

asleep and I didn't want to wake her."

Her hands automatically went to her hair, which was loose, the waves cascading past her shoulders.

"I can't possibly appear at breakfast like this."

"Of course you can." He moved to the bed and scooped her, blankets and all, into his arms and walked out of the room. "We are very casual here at Lark's Song."

He was true to his word. Not only did they sit at a small table near the kitchen by a window overlooking a creek, but also none of the staff acted as if they were surprised at seeing her dressed in only a chemise and a blanket.

Hair disheveled and her face pale, Molly rushed into the room just a few moments later. "I'm so sorry. I overslept." Her eyes widened at seeing Clara's attire. "I will see about your gown straightaway, Miss Clara."

"See about breakfast first," William replied, not giving Clara a chance to speak. "Your mistress is returning to bed as soon as she finishes her breakfast."

Once Molly was out of earshot, Clara leaned forward. "I prefer to dress and see about leaving. My head feels much better and it's best for me to get to my aunt's before anyone gets wind of this." She waved her hand between them. "It's enough to ruin not only my reputation, but affect my sisters as well."

His eyebrows hitched. "Did you actually think you'd get away with sneaking on the property and peering through windows without being found out?"

She lifted and lowered her shoulders while attempting to keep a neutral expression. "Once I verified who was here, which I'm sure you hurried the person away, unfortunately, I would have canceled our engagement."

There was a long pause and Clara narrowed her eyes. He

seemed to be collecting himself to keep from saying the wrong thing.

"It seems to me, Miss Clara, that you are intent on finding a reason to not be engaged to me. Must I remind you that we have announced our engagement formally to London society?"

Clara tried desperately to read him, but a thick wall was erected in seconds. It was an almost physically daunting apparition so impenetrable that she'd never be able to scale it.

He waved away a maid who entered and returned his attention to her. "Once we marry, you can remain in London and away from me. All I will require are children. I don't give much of a care what you do. However, you will not make my family, more precisely, my mother unhappy by terminating this engagement. This is not just about you and your foolish notions."

"I won't be insulted by you keeping a mistress. By your utter disregard of how I appear to everyone by maintaining your relationship so blatantly."

Once again, he seemed to struggle to compose himself. The tightening of his jaw made it obvious he was not having an easy time of it.

"I will tell you everything. I ask that you listen without interrupting."

Clara nodded. "Very well."

WILLIAM STOOD AND went to the window. Dressed as he was, he fit with the scenery behind him. She understood, in that moment, he was meant for living in the country. There, in his small estate, he could relax and spend time doing what he wished without the constant vigilance by London society.

In truth, it was easier to breathe and to have the freedom she had at the moment, like having breakfast in nothing more than a chemise and a blanket.

When he looked at her, there was vulnerability in his gaze. "Five years ago, I visited London frequently, at least monthly. My parents lived in the townhouse and Mother insisted that I do so. Honestly, I love my mother so it was not a hardship. Often, Alexander and I went to the city to enjoy the gentlemen's clubs and keep abreast of what was happening businesswise."

He paused and looked back out the window.

"It was then that I began the assignation with Rachel. I didn't want any formal ties to a woman because I wasn't ready to settle and marry. As you are well aware, in our times, once a man seeks the company of a single woman, it must be with the intention to marry."

Clara itched to ask questions about the reason he sought a woman like Rachel and what had transpired between them lately. But she decided to be patient.

"Then, two years ago," he continued, "I ended things between us. I informed her that I would not be returning to the city as much. My parents moved out here, nearby, and I had no reason to go to London frequently. Honestly, at that point, Rachel had another lover and, although I don't judge her, it was not to my liking. Then again, our relationship, if one can call it that, was only physical."

Heat infused her cheeks and ears, but Clara was determined to learn every detail. "Go on."

"The day you and I appeared together in public for the first time, I was proud to have you on my arm. I suppose I let my guard down. When a footman informed me that one of my horses had been injured, I didn't consider that it should have been my own coachman who should have come to tell me. I was hit from behind, bound and dragged away. When I came to, I was at the wharf. I was released without explanation, but I knew it was Rachel's doing. You see, she was put out that I didn't seek her out after returning."

He took a breath, his wide chest expanding, and released it. "The day I came to see you, I also went to her townhouse to warn her against any other attacks and to ensure she didn't do anything that could affect you. Unfortunately, I believe I fell into her plan. She was prepared. I'm sure a servant was dispatched immediately to see that the gossipmonger would come and witness me being there."

William met her gaze and held it. "Whether you believe me or not, that is the truth."

She believed him. Not only because everything made sense, but also because William was a man of honor. He had no reason to lie. If he wished to continue an affair, there was little she could do to stop him. And no matter how much she'd insinuated at ending their engagement, in truth, they were idle threats.

They would marry. The handsome man before her would be her husband. However, there was one thing she'd not be flexible about.

"I believe you. I'm truly sorry for doubting you. It's just that I'm nervous about all of this. Everything happened so fast."

William sidled next to her and took her hand in his. "I understand. We should make a fresh start of it. You've been cheated out of a courtship. I acted like it was of no importance whether you knew me well or not. Your feelings are important to me, Clara. We can take our time to get to know each other."

He lifted one shoulder. "I find you most beautiful. I suppose the reason I asked you to marry me so suddenly is because if someone else did so first, I'd be forced to kidnap you and prevent it."

"Oh…" Clara knew her eyes were as wide as saucers. "You do?"

William nodded, his warm hand tightening around hers. "Yes. I sound like a barbarian, I know. However, I wouldn't have harmed you. I'd have just kept you long enough to guarantee you would never belong to anyone else."

"I find your narrative disturbing. Hopefully, I would have been able to escape without anyone finding out." Clara couldn't help but giggle at their conversation. "I find you alarmingly handsome. So much so that I can't think straight when you are near." She looked to their joined hands.

Lifting her hand to his lips, William pressed a kiss to her palm. "Will you continue to be my fiancée and marry me, Clara?"

A shiver traveled down her arm and Clara let out a sigh. "Yes, William, I will."

The day turned out to be most delightful. She and William spent hours in front of the fireplace discussing details of the wedding in between telling each other about their likes and dislikes.

Although she could tell he wasn't accustomed to sharing so much, she admired the way he tried his best to answer her questions. Albeit, many times he kept to short replies. He was an elusive, private man and Clara accepted that not everyone was an open book like the members of her family.

She studied him while he scanned a book, searching for a passage to share with her. A frown creasing his brow, he was adorably uncomfortable while scanning the poems in the book she'd handed him.

"It can't be so hard to find a poem to read to me," Clara teased. "It is part of a courtship. To read poetry."

When he raised his gaze to her, it was as if a bolt of lightning hit her. Her entire body shuddered. The effect he had on her was most disconcerting.

William stood and held out his hand.

Unsure what to expect, she took it.

He pulled her to her feet and guided her to move closer until they almost touched. "The poem must be quite scandalous that we have to stand so close." Her breathlessness was surely due to the fall the day before.

Not breaking eye contact, he leaned forward until he pressed his lips to the right side of hers. "You are, by far, one of God's most perfect creations," he whispered and then trailed his mouth to her ear.

Clara shivered.

"Your beauty takes my breath away." His lips lingered just below her ear, the warmth of them ever so delightful.

William didn't touch her, only his mouth and words. And yet, she felt as if she were in the most intimate of lovers' embraces.

Next, he touched his mouth to the side of her neck, just below the jawline. His tongue slipped across her skin so lightly that she wondered if she imagined it. "If I were a dying man, I would cling to life just to look in your eyes one last time." His heated breath fanned over the moist skin and Clara's eyes closed of their own accord and her legs wobbled, threatening to give out.

She reached for him, but he took her hands in his and held them. He took a small step back.

For a long moment, it was silent. But she knew he was

studying her. When she opened her eyes and met his gaze, he smiled.

Before she could wonder what was to come next, he closed the distance between them and pressed a kiss to her lips. It was soft, sweet and undemanding.

"It was your lips that first attracted me. I had to know what you tasted like." He moved to the left side of her throat, and her pulse quickened just as thousands of butterflies took flight in her stomach.

"Oh, my."

He trailed his tongue from her ear down to the base of her neck ever so slowly, stopping along the way to nibble at her tender skin.

Never in her wildest dreams had she known such delight. That the touch of a man's lips would cause her entire being to be so aware of the exact place his mouth lingered.

A soft whimper escaped when his hands cupped her face and lifted it. It was then that he kissed her in a different way, demonstrating the difference between allure and desperate want.

"I pray to remain forever in your favor, my beautiful one," he whispered between kisses.

William's mouth was hot and demanding, his body pressed hard against hers. And yet, it seemed his body was not close enough. Parting her lips to give him more access, she moaned when his tongue invaded. And still, it wasn't enough. The suckling noises and the deep rumbling coming from deep in his chest were like fire. A delightful heat trickled from where his hands slid down her back to the very core of her being and she gasped when it pooled in the most intimate of places.

"Oh!" She gasped for breath and clung to him.

William wrapped his arms around her and held her close. "I am going to go mad waiting for our wedding night, when I can properly take you as my wife." He pressed a kiss to the top of her head. "Did you like my poem?"

How perfect was he? Clara giggled and moved back, hitting his shoulder lightly. "That was not a poem."

"It was. I made it up myself," he said, pretending to be offended.

Clara shook her head. "Very well then, I absolutely loved your poem."

Hopefully, William would make up such poetry often. Especially if each one would make her feel like she did at this moment.

CHAPTER TWELVE

WILLIAM LOOKED ON as Clara studied her cards. It was late afternoon and the coachman was due to return at any moment with the doctor. However, it was definitely a moot point at this time. Clara was well recovered, the bump on the head no more than a nuisance. Fortunately, she and her maid had not left. Instead, they had waited for Jeffrey and then planned to return to London that very day.

He'd wait an additional day before returning quietly to ensure no rumors were spread.

"Miss Clara," Molly gushed as she rushed into the parlor. "Come look. Carriages are coming."

Immediately, Clara's eyes widened. Her mouth fell open and she jumped to her feet, the cards falling from her hands.

"Oh, no!" She raced after Molly to the front windows and William followed.

Sure enough, three carriages moved at a leisurely pace toward the front gates. The first had the Torrington emblem on the door and the second two were unmarked.

His parents. William blew out a breath, unsure of what to think. This was most unexpected. Why would his parents be coming to his estate? And the fact that two additional carriages followed made little sense.

"Is that Clarence?" Molly asked, looking to Clara. "It looks like Clarence."

"Who is Clarence?" William asked, studying the approaching carriages.

Pale and still wide-eyed, Clara turned to him. "Our coachman."

They'd been found out. No doubt, the young man, Jeffrey, had been caught and now the families arrived to either murder him or…what other option was there?

They were already engaged and would soon be wed. Yes, that was it. The wedding was about to take place sooner than expected.

"Oh, goodness," Clara exclaimed. "What should we do? Should I hide?"

He took her by the shoulders and looked into her eyes. "We stand here and greet them. Then we withstand whatever scolding they lash us with. Afterward, you will be taken away by your mother for further reprimand in private."

Her eyes narrowed. "You seem to have everything figured out. How about you go out there and tell them Molly and I left? Then get your coachman to sneak us away while you distract them with stories of my injury."

It was hard not to chuckle. His soon-to-be wife would guarantee that he'd never have a dull moment. Instead, he placed a soft kiss to her lips.

"No. We will face this like adults, my lovely fiancée."

SHE'D NEVER SEEN her mother, father and sisters climb out of a carriage so quickly. Her mother practically raced to the front door.

Knowing it was not the time for formalities, William did away with the need for a servant to open the door. Instead, he and Clara stood just outside the open door awaiting their families.

Her mother scowled at William. Then she looked at Clara, assessing her before glaring at her with pursed lips. "You have some explaining to do."

Behind her mother, Penelope and Vivian hid smiles behind their gloved hands, twinkling eyes going from her to William. They had questions. Clara wanted to laugh. She hadn't any titillating details to give. Although there was the kissing and the fact he'd slept beside the bed, oh and carried her to breakfast...

"Are you listening, Clara?" Her mother's snappy tone made her gasp.

"Yes, Mum, I am," she replied.

Her father had yet to approach. He and William's father seemed to be discussing what to do, heads close as they remained by the coaches. She loved how her handsome father and the duke seemed to get along so well.

Taken by the elbow, she was led inside by her sisters and they all went directly to the parlor. William's mother and hers entered the room, both silently standing side by side.

Immediately, a butler and maid, who'd obviously, been in the third coach, dispatched with their cloaks. They left, offering to bring hot tea.

"Please, sit down." William motioned to the chairs closest to the fireplace. Clara and her sister squeezed into a settee while the mothers each took a chair.

Her mother turned away from Lady Theresa for a moment. "We will wait on your fathers before discussing this distressful situation."

"This is so exciting, isn't it?" Penelope whispered into her ear. "Mother is restraining herself because of the viscount's parents. She kept raising her voice in the carriage. It was so hard for Vivian and me to keep from laughing."

A snort escaped Clara, garnering her a glare from her mother and an inquisitive look from Lady Theresa.

"Stop talking," Clara whispered to Penelope.

Footsteps sounded as the duke, her father and Alexander Yarnsby entered. It seemed wherever Vivian was Mr. Yarnsby was as well. She nudged Vivian with her elbow and her sister returned the gesture, only a bit more forcefully.

The duke met William's gaze. "Son, can you explain to us why you and Miss Clara were here without an escort?"

William stood by the fireplace and slid a glance to Clara. Then he cleared his throat. "It seems Miss Clara found herself in trouble on her way to her aunt's home and…"

This was ridiculous. William was trying to spare her. He wasn't aware that her family would eventually find out the truth. Not because they'd question her until she confessed, but because they never kept anything from one another. It was the Humphries' curse. Keeping any type of secret had always been impossible.

She jumped to her feet. "Thank you, William, but I will tell it better." Clara offered him a weak smile before facing the mothers. "I came to spy on him because I thought he'd brought that horrible woman, Rachel Witting, here. Unfortunately, I fell off a pile of wood and injured myself."

She waited for her mother's hitched breathing to regulate.

"I planned to go directly to Aunt Bettina's home once I'd satisfied my curiosity. However, Molly lost her balance and fell on top of me, knocking me unconscious."

There were several gasps. Clara wasn't sure if it was the

fact she'd passed out or that she'd been spying. It could also be that she'd spoken out loud about William's lover. She let out a breath and tried to figure out which part she should have left out.

"Yes…well, and why did you remain here?" Her father, bless him, looked about to fall over.

She looked to William who lifted a brow in return. Now wasn't the time for him to stop speaking. It was his turn to explain that he'd insisted she remain due to her serious injury.

Seeming to finally take the hint, he nodded. "As she said, she was unconscious. I insisted she remain here until a doctor was brought."

This time, it was her mother who spoke. "And why was Jeffrey sent to the market, where he was caught by Clarence trying to convince Jules to pretend to be a doctor?"

Clara almost laughed at her family's abilities to get facts. They were much better than any London investigator.

When William gave her an incredulous look, she realized this was news to him as well. She and Moly had made a mess of things.

"I didn't wish to worry you." Clara pointed to Molly who shrunk back from the doorway. "It was Molly's idea."

"Don't drag that poor girl into this," her father said with an uncharacteristic snarl. "You have caused us a great deal of worry and embarrassment with your thoughtless actions."

At his scolding, her face burned with embarrassment and she could only look at the floor. At her sides, both sisters stiffened. When Albert Humphries got angry, everyone took note. The normally mild-mannered man usually allowed his wife to be the disciplinarian.

"Therefore," he continued, "if the viscount's family will still have you, a wedding must take place immediately. I do not trust you to stay out of mischief." He looked to William. "I hope you are aware of what you're getting in to."

"Albert!" her mother cried out. "That was not necessary." She looked to Lady Theresa. "I'm so sorry. This is most distressful."

Lady Torrington threw her head back and laughed. "Honestly, this is not as bad as it seems. I don't blame you, dear," she said to Clara. "I once followed the duke on horseback to ensure he was not lying about a destination. Unfortunately, I found myself in the middle of a fox hunt."

Clara wanted to laugh but, after a warning look from her mother, she only smiled and nodded. Penelope, however, wasn't as deterred. She giggled without care.

Unfazed, Lady Torrington continued, "I think you are just what William needs, dear girl. A wife who will keep him on his toes."

"I agree," the duke added and turned his attention to his son. "You must see about a special license. William, you and Alexander must ride to London immediately. We will have a wedding before news spreads."

William looked to Clara and then back at the gathered parents. "May I speak to Clara in private for a moment?"

"No," all four parents said at once.

Clara wasn't sure, but it seemed as if Alexander stifled a chuckle and tried to cover it up with a cough. Both her sisters' lips were pressed together.

"Very well. Then I will be on my way." He gave Clara a look she couldn't decipher. Was it a "you'll be fine" look? Or perhaps, it was a "now you've done it" look. She decided he conveyed more of a "don't worry, I'll return as soon as I can" look.

"TELL US EVERYTHING." That night, Penelope draped herself across the bed, her eyes focused on Clara's face.

"Don't leave out even the tiniest of details," Vivian added. Her older sister sat on a chair by the hearth, her clutched hands up against her chin.

Clara practically pranced as she paced across the room. Her sisters' undivided attention tracked ever single step.

"There isn't really much to tell, but I will do my best. My heart thundered as if it were about to burst out of my chest as the carriage neared the gates of Lark's Song..."

CHAPTER THIRTEEN

"WITH THIS RING, I thee wed…" William's deep voice was the only sound in the room. His gaze locked with Clara's, he slid the golden ring onto her shaky finger.

Clara tore her eyes away to look at the young clergyman who, by his moist upper lip and brow, was just as nervous as she was. He'd been the only one available as the older priest was very ill and had taken to bed.

It wasn't every day a young priest from a small town was called in to marry a duke's son.

When it was Clara's turn to say the vows, she managed to get through them without bursting into tears. Not because she was afraid or anything of that sort, but because she'd always imagined her wedding day to be more focused on things like flowers and food and not so much on her.

This was, indeed, a special day. Her sisters had brought a new dress for her to wear and the veil she donned was her mother's. Since it was much too cold for flowers, Lady Torrington had brought a rosary and a small, beautiful bible to hold.

William was most handsome in his dark coat and cream cravat. The colors set off his dark hair and bright, gray eyes. Standing next to him, she felt protected and safe. It was as if by marrying him, she had never to fear anything.

She closed her eyes, listening to the sounds of the young priest's words and inhaling the scent of William. He smelled of pine and outdoors, uniquely masculine and oh so perfect.

Finally, the priest pronounced them husband and wife. Much to her delight, the young man didn't pass out before announcing they could kiss.

Clara lifted her face to William, her eyelids falling.

The kiss was perfect. It was soft enough not to cause their mothers anxiety and he ended it with a soft, quick nip that made her insides tingle.

Hand in hand, they turned to face their families.

Both mothers wiped away tears and their fathers tried to clumsily calm them. Penelope and Vivian clapped and smiled widely, as did Molly who stood just behind them. Alexander Yarnsby watched from the side without expression, hooded eyes locked on them.

"Let us go to the dining room, shall we?" Lady Theresa led the way.

They were at the Torringtons' country home now. Everyone had relocated to the larger home from William's smaller estate while he and Alexander were in London.

It was a beautiful home and Clara itched to explore it once she lived at Lark's Song.

At the thought, she frowned and nibbled her lip. With everything happening so fast, she'd yet to have a discussion with William regarding their living arrangements and her refusal to remain in London.

No matter, there was time yet.

Everyone was invited to toast, even the staff. Clara was delighted that Molly was more of a guest as she wore a beautiful, simple gown that Clara had bought her for her birthday earlier that year.

The frock was not expensive, but much nicer than most of Molly's clothes. In truth, all three sisters always ensured the staff received nice gifts and items they normally could not afford.

"You're not here, are you?" William whispered into her ear as they made their way to the dining room.

Clara slid a glance to him. "I was thinking of something we must discuss later."

"Interesting. My mind is entirely on later as well. However, discussion is not part of it."

It was impossible to keep her eyes from rounding and she inhaled sharply. "I forgot about that. Goodness, I hope you plan to instruct me as to what to do."

This time, it was William's eyes that grew wide. "We will talk about it later."

She let out a long sigh. "Very well."

THE NEWLYWEDS ARRIVED by carriage to Lark's Song with only Molly, the cook and her husband, the stable hand.

It had been a long day and, by all accounts, she should be exhausted. Instead, Clara's body tingled with anticipation of what the evening would bring.

Once in the bedroom, Clara hurried to prepare for bed. "Do you have any idea what I should do?" she asked Molly. The maid shook her head.

"No, Miss Clara. I have no idea. I think you should definitely not move. I hear it's a woman's duty to endure whatever her husband does." The maid looked to the doorway. "Will you please tell me everything tomorrow?"

Clara blushed. "I suppose I can. And I will tell my sisters

as well. Women shouldn't go into this blind. Mother gasped when I asked her about it. I'm shocked she didn't tell me anything."

"You did ask rather publicly," Molly replied as she untied Clara's dress. "I am not sure it was something to be discussed in mixed company."

"True. However, I did expect she'd spirit me away and speak about it. Instead, she was like a turtle, hiding in its shell."

Moments later, the door opened and Clara did her best to keep from hyperventilating. Her heart beat rather fast and the butterflies that had insisted on swirling suddenly turned into some sort of floppy mass that sat at the bottom of her belly like a stone.

William studied her for a moment. She lay in the bed like a porcelain doll on display. Molly had pulled her hair back away from her face, tied only with a ribbon so that it fell down her back.

There was a serene lift to the corners of his lips. Although she wanted to seem unfazed, Clara couldn't form anything close to a smile.

What if he was about to hurt her in a way that was too horrible for words? Was that the reason mothers always cried at weddings and couldn't share what would transpire? Instead, they offered words that didn't quite encourage their daughters while at the same time not discouraging either.

"Come." William held out his hand. "How about we have a bit of brandy and discuss the day."

Glad for the reprieve, Clara scrambled from the bed, almost tripping on her nightgown. "I thought you said discussion wasn't part of the night's plan."

He handed her a small glass and watched on as she sipped.

The warmth of the alcohol was heavenly as it slid down her throat.

"We make the brandy at my family's home. My great-grandfather always had an affinity for good brandy. He found out what was needed and we've continued to make it for many years." She watched as he took a drink. Then he put the glass down and removed his coat and cravat.

His darkened gaze met hers. "I know today wasn't exactly the wedding you probably dreamed of. We can have a reception once we return to London," he continued as he put the coat over the back of a chair. When he turned, his wide back took her attention. He was a large man, wide of shoulders and chest. Slender at the hips and, from what she could tell, his legs were muscular.

"A reception would be wonderful. When do you think we'll return to London?"

They spoke of engagements they'd been invited to and which were best to attend. As he spoke, he drank his brandy and waited for her to also drink.

When her glass was empty, he refilled it.

Clara took a breath. "I will have to insist that I not remain in London. If you return to Lark's Song, I will do so as well. I refused to be an abandoned wife."

"I think Mother was correct in stating you are the perfect match for me. Has there ever been a boring time when you or your sisters are involved?" He neared as he spoke, his gaze boring into hers. His eyes were darker than she'd ever seen them.

She was fascinated at how her body warmed to his perusal, leaning forward of its own accord. When he leaned forward to press a slow kiss onto her mouth, her eyes closed of their own volition.

No. She needed to be mindful of what he did. It would not do. Whatever magic he held over her must be due to him being her husband. That was something no one had warned her about either.

"Oh, my," Clara said, letting out a shuddering breath when his tongue trailed down the side of her neck. At the same time, his hands encircled her waist. The warm of them seeped through her nightdress.

"Clara, open your eyes." His hoarse whisper startled her and her eyes popped open.

He watched her and smiled. William had a beautiful smile. If she were the swooning type, Clara would be rendered unconscious at seeing it.

"Kiss me," he commanded. "Put your arms around my neck, press your body against mine and kiss me."

"Very well then. I have to put this down." She turned away, drank the last bit of brandy and put the glass down on a small side table.

William stood straight, his eyes on her. He was much too tall, so she had to lift to her tiptoes. Then she lifted her arms and wrapped them around his neck. The second part was a bit scandalous, but she was determined to do everything perfectly. Her body fell against his and she gasped at how intimate it felt. For whatever reason, this was nothing like the other day when they'd kissed.

He was solid, immobile and the sensation of her breasts against his chest was startling. His hard hips pressed into her and just under his stomach was hard and solid. Her eyes latched on to his lips. She wanted them tasting, nibbling and licking hers.

However, he'd instructed she should be the one to kiss him. So she threaded her fingers through his hair and pulled his head down. Then she took his mouth with hers, pressing her lips against his and trailing soft kisses from one side to the other. William relaxed against her, his mouth softening, but he did not return her kiss.

An idea struck. She sucked on his bottom lip and nibbled on it. His breath caught and she was delighted to have finally had an effect on him. Encouraged, she continued and then, ever so slowly, she pushed her tongue between his lips.

His reaction made her giddy. His arms wrapped around her and he came to life, returning the kiss by suckling on her tongue and returned her mouth with so much passion, she could've sworn it had to be what heaven would feel like.

They continued kissing and he lifted her into his arms, carrying her to the bed. Clara wanted to be nervous, but she wanted to keep kissing more.

He leaned over her. "Don't move."

Although he only took a step or two back, Clara wanted to whimper in protest. She couldn't draw her eyes away as he undressed. William didn't seem to mind as he quickly dispatched his boots, shirt and pants. Then he was totally and utterly nude.

"Is that how you're going to sleep?" Clara focused on the member that stuck out from his body in the most interesting fashion.

He nodded and moved closer. "And so are you."

"I am?"

"Yes." He pulled her forward. "Lift your arms."

She did and he pulled her gown off.

"Now, we're both naked," she pointed out the obvious, too interested in his body to notice he regarded her in return. "It's cold. You should get under the blankets."

What she found most peculiar was how much she desired

him to be under the blankets with her. She desired to touch his skin and press against it. Oh, goodness, this had to be part of the ritual. Then when she least expected it, the enduring would begin.

However, he climbed on the bed without moving the coverings. He loomed over her. "I am going to make you mine now, Clara. Allow me to love you like no other."

She wasn't sure what to say. It didn't matter much as he covered her mouth with his and her ability to speak was utterly forgotten.

When his hand slid over her skin, it left a trail of heat that fueled every inch of her. The intensity grew until she clung to him as if her life depended on it.

The instant he took her, Clara cried out and wondered how it was possible for pain and passion to mix in such a way.

William took her to heights that she could never describe until she gave up any hope of clinging to reality and fell into an abyss of stars and clouds.

Her entire being became his as he showed her how love-making was accomplished. As much as she tried to keep her mind clear so that she could recite what happened later, all thought evaporated with every kiss.

Each exclamation and sound was like a symphony. The final note was William's hoarse cry when he finally reached his release.

THERE WAS A strange heat surrounding him and William fought to open his eyes. Whatever it was did not bother him. Actually, it was soothing and somewhat alluring.

Clara. His eyes flew open. It was the first time he'd spent an entire night with a woman. Normally, his sexual activity had been casual, with him leaving afterwards.

His spirited bride was fast asleep, her breathing even. Head on her pillow facing him, her lips were pursed as if expecting to be kissed. Although he couldn't see the rest of her, he'd done his best to touch every inch of her delectable body the night before.

From the waist down she was pressed against him, one leg thrown across his thighs. It prevented him from sliding away without waking her and he wondered if the minx did it on purpose.

He couldn't help but smile. There really was no reason to get up he considered and allowed his eyes to close again.

CHAPTER FOURTEEN

"I T'S LOVELY TO see you, dear," Lady Barrow exclaimed, kissing Clara on both cheeks. They were at her family's home. It was two weeks after being wed and Clara had been summoned for tea.

It was close to Christmas and there was much planning to do if they were to have a holiday gathering and wedding celebration.

"I do think we should have it here," Penelope said, her face bright at the fact she was included.

"Nonsense," her mother replied. "It's much too small. We will pay for a ballroom."

"I insist it be held at my house," Lady Barrow offered. "We can both be hostesses."

Her mother smiled widely, but then frowned at the knock on the front door. The butler hurried by. "Who could that be?"

It was Glenda, Clara's cousin and good friend. The young woman hurried in and stopped when she noticed Lady Barrow. "I'm so sorry. I came to see Clara. I hate to interrupt."

"Don't be silly, darling." Her mother motioned to a chair at the table next to Clara. "Sit."

Glenda's green eyes were bright, a sure tell she had a juicy tidbit of gossip to impart. Penelope, Vivian and Clara exchanged looks, silently trying to come up with a plan to get away so they could speak privately.

They knew Glenda would not say a thing in front of Lady Barrow.

Their mother, however, knew Glenda well as she'd visited often since childhood. "Go on, Glenda, please share what it is you've learned."

"It's actually something a bit sad."

"Oh, no." Clara took her friend's hand. "What is it? Is someone hurt?"

Lady Barrow looked on with obvious worry. "Please go on."

Glenda gave Clara an apologetic look. "It seems Rachel Witting is dead."

The room was silent. Clara wasn't sure what to say. The woman had no close friends as far as anyone knew. "What happened?"

"She was found dead in her bed. My mother's maid was at the bakery when she overheard someone come to get Mrs. Witting's cook."

"That is horrible. To die alone." Sarah shook her head.

"If she was alone," Penelope quipped and then covered her mouth with both hands.

Other than a glare, her mother refrained from saying anything in return.

"Should I remain and help?" Glenda offered, giving Clara a soft smile. "I'm so excited about your reception. It will almost make up for not inviting me to the wedding."

The mood in the room changed as everyone began to plan the elaborate event. Clara could not stop the excitement that bubbled inside her. Even the knowledge of the death would not keep her from enjoying the afternoon.

"I have something to announce," Vivian said, her tone a strange high pitch.

Every eye turned to her and she smiled at them.

"Did you eat something sour?" Penelope asked. "Your smile looks a bit strange."

"Oh, hush." Clara tapped Penelope's arm. "What is it, Vivian?"

Her sister straightened. "I will be attending the wedding ball with Lord Jameson as my escort."

Clara's eyes popped wide while her mother and Lady Barrow both froze with teacups held midair.

"Why?" Penelope was the first to find her voice. "He is plainer than a potato and has the personality of one."

"Goodness," Lady Barrow exclaimed with a chuckle. "That is definitely a most appropriate description of the poor boy."

Vivian stood. "Because he is the only one that dared ask. The only man who made it past my most irritating constant guard."

"You should speak to Mr. Yarnsby," Penelope stated with a stern nod. "If he is not going to court you, then he should not be in the way of you finding a suitable suitor."

Their mother held up a hand. "Now, let's not be harsh. I'm sure Lord Jameson is a fine young man. We should allow Vivian to make her own choice in this matter."

"I should go." Glenda jumped to her feet, but then plopped back down when Clara's mother yanked her by the arm.

Sarah Humphries did not mind Glenda's propensity for gossip except when it came to her family. "You will remain until the urge to repeat what was just said is gone. If anyone repeats that we think Lord Jameson looks like a potato, I will personally pluck every hair from your head."

Glenda gasped and Clara had to take several deep breaths to keep from bursting out laughing.

FINALLY, SEVERAL HOURS later, every detail of the ball was planned. It would be at least a week before they'd have flowers, music and the menu completed, but as far as dates and such, it was all done.

Lady Barrow and Clara's mother were ecstatic at the prospect of planning the grandest ball of the season, while Clara was most interested in showing off her very handsome husband.

Her father and cousin, Todd, arrived just as she was leaving and she was glad to see them both. Clara hugged both, noting that another carriage had just pulled up.

"I believe that is Mr. Yarnsby," Todd said in a flat tone. "He and I will be discussing a business proposition."

Clara narrowed her eyes. "Is that so?"

He lifted a brow. "Yes, that is so."

She turned to glance over her shoulder at Vivian who scowled at them. "Todd, what are you doing? Why would you have business with him?"

Instead of a reply, Todd turned to look out the door. "Oh look, here he comes now."

Clara smiled at the handsome man when he entered. "Will you join us for dinner tonight, Alexander?"

"I will be there," he replied, his green eyes sparkling.

"Very well." Clara looked to her mother and Lady Barrow, who watched the interactions with unabashed enjoyment. Glenda was about to burst, but had yet to leave her seat. Now, with this new occurrence, she'd probably be there all night. She definitely took Clara's mother's threats very seriously.

As Clara left her parents' home, she couldn't help the smile that stretched across her face.

"Where to, Lady Torrington?" the coachman asked.

"Home, Samuel."

It was just at that moment that Clara realized her home was no longer where her parents lived, but where William was.

THE TORRINGTON GALA was the talk of London society. Anyone who was of note attended the soiree that evening. The Barrows' grand ballroom was filled to capacity. Guests spilled over into the smaller parlors and out to the wide balconies. Every guest was there to pay their respects to Clara and William, ensuring to be in their good graces.

Tones of the first waltz began and William, who looked splendid in head-to-toe black, led Clara, who wore a soft pink gown, to the center of the room.

He bowed over her hand and she couldn't help a blush as she lowered into a deep curtsy. The song commenced and as he twirled her across the gleaming floor, Clara's skirts swooshed around her legs when he brought her around full circle.

"I didn't know so many would attend," Clara said, her voice breathless. "They want to secure invites in the future from us or the Barrows."

William arched a brow. "I wonder how many will travel to Lark's Song."

At his mention of the country estate, her stomach lurched. It would be Christmas in another week and, although she'd made plans for dinner at her parents' home as well as hosting at the Torrington townhouse, they'd yet to speak about their plans for the New Year.

If she were to be honest, she didn't wish to ruin the holidays by pondering about it, so she'd not brought it up to William.

However, this was too much of an opportunity to miss. She let out a sigh. "I suppose I can host a party or two at the townhouse and, come spring, I will ensure to host a large gathering so that my sisters can have a proper season."

"What about Lark's Song?" he asked with a scowl.

"First of all, no one will travel that far. And secondly, I can't plan something there while living here."

"You're not living here." He guided her around another couple. "I want you with me."

Clara smiled broadly. "Is that so? Since when Viscount Torrington?"

The way he flattened his lips, it appeared she was forcing food he didn't like down his throat.

"I wished for a wife that would do as she was told, bear me children and remain in London so I could continue to live peacefully in the countryside. However, I find that now my wish has changed. I didn't expect to feel this way."

Her breath caught. "How do you feel, William?"

This time, his face softened and his warm gaze locked with hers. "As if I cannot breathe unless you're with me."

"Oh." She stepped on his foot and then stumbled as her legs turned to jelly. "Goodness, I'm so sorry."

"What did you wish for, Clara?" He spoke softly against her ear and then pressed a lingering kiss to the sensitive skin just below it. Her husband knew her weakness. So she gave him a knowing look.

"I wished for my sister, Vivian, to find a good husband. I never wished for much for myself until I met you. I wish for you to be my dark prince forever."

There were gasps as he stopped them from dancing and took her mouth with his.

As usual, everything disappeared until there was only him.

EXCERPT OF
THE SEDUCTION OF MR. YARNSBY

CHAPTER ONE

London, England – December 1817

"HAPPY CHRISTMAS!" THE Humphries family gathered at the doorway of their London home to welcome the visitors.

Giddy with excitement, Vivian Humphries could barely stand still. It was to be a wonderful holiday because her sister Clara was in London spending Christmas day with the family.

Standing in the doorway beside Clara was her husband, the dashing Viscount William Torrington, along with his parents, Duke and Duchess Torrington.

Welcomes and kisses on the cheeks were exchanged as the group entered and were greeted by Vivian, her parents, and her sister Penelope. All together it was a mad jumble, and she loved every second of it.

Just behind the group, the most maddening man stood and was obviously there to visit as well.

Like a brother to William, Mr. Alexander Yarnsby was included in everything. Of course, it shouldn't have surprised Vivian he was there. She took a deep breath, deciding not to allow his appearance to dampen her good spirits.

Forcing her smile to remain, Vivian slid a look to Penelope, her youngest sister. As expected, Penelope had no qualms whatsoever at showing her displeasure at Alexander Yarnsby's appearance, glaring at the man.

"We are pleased that you are joining us today," her mother, ever gracious, told Yarnsby as he bent over her hand, kissing the back of it.

Just as his green eyes met hers, Vivian took a step back. "I do believe Cook calls." She began to turn, but Penelope took advantage of the announcement.

"I will go and see what she needs." Her sister dashed away, taking with her an opportunity for Vivian to ignore the ever-overwhelming Mr. Yarnsby.

"Miss Humphries. It is a pleasure, as always." His deep voice was like a smooth velvet. At least to Vivian it was. He didn't seem to have the same effect on anyone else in her family.

Since her mother looked on, she held up her hand, and he took it. "Mr. Yarnsby."

"Isn't it wonderful we have a houseful at Christmas?" her mother exclaimed to someone. Vivian wasn't sure who, as her attention was riveted to where Mr. Yarnsby's lips lingered on her hand.

"Vivian?" Her mother studied her. "Why don't you and your sisters slip into the parlor?"

Apparently, she'd forgotten to breathe because she gulped in air, alarmed to have lost herself for a moment. Thankfully, Yarnsby was already walking away with the other men to her father's study.

How long had she been standing there like a statue with her hand in the air? It was most mortifying and the reason she disliked being anywhere near the annoying Mr. Yarnsby.

There was a knowing smile playing on the edges of her mother's lips when she looked at her.

"Would you like to see the preparations in the dining room?" her mother asked Duchess Torrington, and they left. Her mother wanted time alone with Her Grace as they'd become fast friends and liked to coordinate the social events they'd attend.

"I would think Mr. Yarnsby would be spending the holiday with his own family," Vivian announced as soon as she entered the sitting room. "I find the man most distracting. He does everything in his power to annoy me."

Clara's expression became pensive. "I do believe that he and William have spent the holidays together since they were very young." There was more to the story, but it was not something Vivian truly cared to speak about. He'd already distracted her enough for the day.

"I truly hope Tommy comes tonight. I wish to discuss becoming engaged." Penelope sighed dramatically. She was enamored with the idea of marrying her childhood friend Thomas Rutherford, who presently worked as an understudy at Parliament.

Clara's eyes widened. "You must not do such a thing," Clara chided. "It is most inappropriate to bring up the subject of marriage with someone who has not declared himself."

"I agree," Vivian added. "A lady should not have to ask a man to declare himself."

"Very well. I am sure he will make his intentions clear soon. It is just that he is very busy." Penelope looked out to the garden and once again sighed.

Vivian took her young sister's hand. "It is not that we do not wish you to be happy. However, we do not wish you ruined by your own actions."

"I find the confines of society utterly suffocating. However, your statements have merit," Penelope agreed with a pout.

To keep from laughing, Vivian bit her lip. The youngest, while a delight, was proving to be as adventurous in nature as Clara. Both of her sisters often disguised themselves by borrowing the maid's clothing to go about town on whatever outlandish adventure called to them.

As much as Vivian agreed with some of the things they did, she'd always been more reserved. The curse of being the eldest and feeling responsible for them, she supposed.

"Ladies," Gerard, the butler, stood at the doorway. "Misters Rutherford and Jameson are here."

Her stomach dipped and her breath caught. "Oh goodness, I'd forgotten that I mentioned Christmas dinner to Mr. Jameson," Vivian said, jumping to her feet. "I must inform Mother."

As she dashed from the room, Penelope's voice was loud. "This will be a most enjoyable Christmas, will it not?"

"Mother?" Vivian entered the kitchen to find only the cook and another cook's maid, along with Mary, her companion, and Molly, Clara's companion, scurrying about.

"Your mother and Duchess Torrington have gone to the sitting room," Molly said, rushing to her. They embraced. "I miss you so, Miss Vivian."

"I miss you as well," Vivian replied, meaning it.

She hurried to her mother's small sitting room to find the two women, each with a cup of tea, at ease with each other's company. "Mother, Mr. Jameson is here, and Tommy has also arrived."

"Oh dear," her mother said, immediately getting to her feet. "I will have to direct that two more place settings be added." She hurried from the room, leaving Vivian with Duchess Torrington.

Theresa Torrington was a striking, youthful woman with hazel almond-shaped eyes and a bright expression. She gave the illusion of being much younger than her true age, a number Vivian did not venture to guess.

"Come sit, Vivian," Duchess Torrington said, motioning to the chair her mother had just vacated. "We have never had the opportunity to get to know each other privately have we?."

"I am pleased that you and your husband came tonight," Vivian said, sitting. "She purposefully left out Mr. Yarnsby's unexpected presence.

The woman smiled brightly. "We were delighted that the invitation was extended. We expected a quiet evening at home with only Alex for company."

"Yes, well, we could not allow it," Vivian said. "We look forward to seeing you and your family whenever you come to London." She looked to the doorway. "When you return to the country, will Mr. Yarnsby go as well?"

With a delighted chuckle, Duchess Torrington patted her hand. "Of course. Is he not lovely? I do hope that you or your younger dear sister catch his eye. I do love Alex and wish for him to be happy."

Why would the arrogant man not be happy? In Vivian's opinion, if the man was alone, it was his own doing.

"I am not sure that he will consider either of us. He seems preoccupied with . . . himself." Vivian stopped speaking at her unfortunate choice of words.

Once again Duchess Torrington laughed as Vivian covered her cheeks in mortification.

"I did not mean to say he is self-absorbed. Oh dear, what I mean is that he seems to prefer his own company." It didn't sound much better; there was nothing to do that would erase her gaffe.

"Do not worry, dear, I will keep this between us." Duchess Torrington became pensive. "Alexander is naturally reserved, which can at times be off-putting. You must believe me when I say that he is the least arrogant person ever. When you get to know him, you will agree."

"I do apologize," Vivian started. "He is part of your family, and the last thing I wish to do is to speak ill. It is the way of the Humphries to have a hard time curtailing our tongues."

"Which is what makes each of you so delightful."

Thankfully, her mother returned and took Duchess Torrington's attention. "Everything is prepared and settled. Let us go to the dining room. I believe the gentlemen are already there."

Upon arriving at the dining room, Clara and Penelope met them at the doorway. The men stood and held out chairs. Vivian wasn't sure where to look. While she wished to greet Mr. Jameson, she hoped to avoid looking at Mr. Yarnsby.

"Miss Vivian," Melvin Jameson said in greeting. His hand on the back of a chair, he motioned for her to sit.

"I am pleased that you accepted my invitation. I did not expect you'd be free," Vivian replied, smiling at him. Melvin Jameson had never lost the plumpness from youth. He had a cherubic face that was not unpleasant to look upon. The slight lift to the corner of his lips gave the impression of being continuously in good spirits. With dark eyes and overly pink lips, he reminded Vivian of youths in Rubenesque paintings. Melvin was the likeable sort that everyone felt at ease around.

A total contradiction to Mr. Yarnsby, who stood on her left side.

Vivian slid a glance past Melvin to Clara, who was having

a horrible time keeping from smiling. Narrowing her eyes, Vivian pinned her youngest sister, who sat next to family friend, Tommy, across the table from her.

Penelope gave her an impish smile. "You should sit."

"Yes, of course." Vivian allowed Mr. Jameson to assist and settled between the two men. Of course, it was her sisters' doing, they must have sneaked in and rearranged things. They lived for opportunities like this. It would be the topic of discussion after the meal.

Or perhaps, her mother had done it after all, seating was assigned by her. She'd managed to slip in two additional people without upsetting the decorum that was required.

Her mother sat at the head of the table, Vivian's father at the foot. To his right was Duchess Torrington, on his left Clara. Mr. Yarnsby sat between Clara and Vivian, and to Vivian's left was Mr. Jameson.

At her mother's right, given his elevated status, was the Duke of Torrington. On her mother's left was her new son-in-law, William, Clara's husband. Penelope and Thomas were seated across from Vivian, between William and Duchess Torrington.

With there being five people on Vivian's side of the table, she could scarcely move her arms without touching either of the men.

The clinking of glasses brought everyone's attention to her father, who welcomed the visitors and motioned for the servants to serve the meal.

Once the meal was served, everyone began conversing. Vivian turned away from Mr. Yarnsby to speak to Mr. Jameson, but unfortunately, he had been pulled into a conversation with the duke and her mother.

"Is it not wonderful that Tommy could join us tonight?"

Penelope exclaimed, smiling brightly at her companion. Thomas Rutherford gave her and indulgent look, seeming pleased at her attention. He didn't seem in the least enamored, but he looked on her as if appreciating a sister.

"It seems your duties at Parliament have kept you away from us for much too long," Vivian said. "Penelope does miss you horribly."

Her father cleared his throat. "It is important that Tommy become acquainted with the gentlemen of good station there. Do you agree, Mr. Yarnsby?"

"I have little understanding of all the goings on at Parliament. I would imagine that anyone wishing to have a career in politics should apply themselves completely. Things seems to change constantly, depending on moods."

Clara chuckled with delight. "I do wonder at times what drives certain decisions."

Their father gave Clara a pointed look. "The running of our country is a serious matter."

Vivian huffed softly. "Does lawmaking not interest you Mr. Yarnsby?"

"As it affects my businesses and my family's estate, it has to."

"And yet you have no confidence in the system?"

Tommy leaned forward. "If I may ask Mr. Yarnsby, have you attended any sessions to observe? You may find it enlightening."

"I have, in fact, and plan to attend several times in the upcoming weeks. Perhaps I will seek you out?"

"If I may be of any assistance, do not hesitate."

"Tommy is not only a wonderful friend, but quite intelligent as well," Vivian bragged.

Her father nodded, looking to Duchess Torrington.

"Tommy has been about our home since wearing short trousers. A very dear friend of the family. I must agree with Vivian; he is indeed most intelligent."

Tommy beamed at the compliments. He was a dear.

"What of you, Miss Vivian, what takes your interests?" Yarnsby asked, his eyes locked with hers.

"Currently, I have been helping Father in his research of the resocialization of those held prisoner or captured for long periods back into society. It is most fascinating."

"Where would one find these subjects to study? A stroll about the pier or the underbellies of London streets?"

It was hard to tell if he made jest or was serious. Vivian tore her gaze from his and turned to her father. "Father, can you explain to Mr. Yarnsby where subjects for your current study are found?"

Delighted to speak about his current subject, her father embarked on an explanation. Vivian snuck a look to her mother, who continuously scolded them about bringing the subject up.

Thankfully, she was entertained by the duke, so she'd not noticed.

A sharp kick made her look to Penelope, who motioned to Clara.

Her sister had somehow turned the conversation away from captured people to Vivian. "Vivian is an avid birdwatcher and enjoys spending time with a group that splits their time between Hyde Park and excursions to the countryside."

She wanted to gawk at her sister. Hoping to find a new hobby, Vivian had joined a bird-watching group and attended their excursions only twice. The birdwatchers had turned out to be the most boring group of people she'd ever come across. Why was Clara bringing it up?

"Then you must join me and Mr. Yarnsby next week," Duchess Torrington exclaimed with a bright smile. "You will be enthralled at the wonderful assortment of birds often spotted around our estate. We have spied waxwings and fieldfares, and on occasion, even a chiffchaff."

Vivian had no idea what Duchess Torrington had just described; she knew little to nothing about birds. However, there was no way to get out of the invitation. She'd already agreed to go to her sister and William's country home for the winter, and therefore she was now obliged to do whatever it was one did when birding.

"I would be delighted. I am certain it will be enthralling."

Duchess Torrington looked to Yarnsby. Vivian forced her head to turn in his direction. "Alex, did you hear? Miss Vivian is fond of bird-watching."

Something about the way he studied her made Vivian shrink back. "I agree, you must absolutely join Aunt Theresa and myself." Obviously, he considered Duchess Torrington his aunt, despite not being related.

"Ah…yes, well, I will do my best."

Clara yelped when Vivian pinched her. She managed to cover it up with a soft laugh. "I am so thrilled that my sisters will be with me for at least part of the winter."

"I wasn't aware you planned to leave for the season," Mr. Jameson said. He looked perturbed, his brows lifted. "Was I wrong to presume you would be attending the New Year's Gala with me?"

For a moment Vivian was caught off guard by the annoyed tone. Had she agreed to attend the gala? The last time they'd spoken, he'd brought up so many topics, it made her head swim.

"My family has been planning this for several weeks. I will

not return until after the New Year, I'm afraid."

With a huff, he shook his head disapprovingly. "We will speak of it later."

"Do not be put out. There will be plenty of festivities after the New Year," Vivian replied, feeling badly that she'd perhaps misled the poor man.

Instead of a reply, he gave a one-shouldered shrug. At the gesture, Penelope rolled her eyes and turned to Tommy. "I wish you were going to the country with me."

Tommy tapped her sister's hand. "My days of leisure are over for now. We have to forge separate lives now, poppet."

Penelope's eyes bulged at the pet name usually reserved for when someone considered another childish or immature. Vivian coughed in an attempt to distract from the interaction.

"I am not a poppet," Penelope exclaimed. "Why did you call me that?"

Used to his youngest daughter's dramatics, their father stood. "If everyone would be so kind as to remove to the parlor now"—he motioned to the doors—"I believe my wife has some entertainment planned."

Once again, Mr. Jameson stood and assisted with her chair. When she turned away, Vivian found herself face-to-face with Mr. Yarnsby. His gaze lowered to her lips, then quickly darted away to Jameson.

After a soft nod, he turned to escort Clara out of the room.

Something was afoot, but Vivian could not put her finger on it. It was useless to try to get Penelope's attention as she walked past on Tommy's arm with her nose in the air. Tommy was apologizing profusely, although it was evident he wasn't sure what he'd done wrong.

"My mother calls me poppet at times," he explained.

Penelope glared at him.

"May I have a word?" Mr. Jameson asked while pulling Vivian aside.

She met his gaze. "Very well. Just for a moment. We cannot linger."

When his hand covered hers, Vivian wanted to pull it away. Of course, she'd known the man was interested in courting her, and at first she'd been agreeable to it. But the more she got to know Melvin Jameson, the more Vivian regretted ever accepting his company.

There was something about him that gave her pause. At the same time, there wasn't any cause for her to be reluctant. Melvin was from a good, established family and was well liked in society.

Her father liked him, and even her cousin Todd, who disliked everyone, often met with Melvin at the gentlemen's club.

"I had hoped to invite you to come to my house for supper—along with your parents, of course. I wish to formalize my desire to court—"

"Vivian?" Clara appeared, her gaze moving from her to Mr. Jameson. "Ah, there you are. We cannot possibly commence without you."

With more force than called for, Vivian snatched her hands away from Mr. Jameson and practically ran past Clara into the parlor.

About the Author

Most days, USA Today Bestseller Hildie McQueen can be found in her overly-tight leggings and green hoodie, holding a cup of tea while stalking the lawn guy. In the afternoons, she browses the Internet for semi-nude men to post on Facebook.

Being a full-time writer is no joke. The co-workers are dogs, no one cleans the office and the only human contact is usually carrying a package and in a hurry to leave.

Author Hildie McQueen loves unusual situations and getting into interesting adventures, which is what her characters do as well. She writes romance because she is in love with love! Author of historical and contemporary romances, she writes something every reader can enjoy.

Hildie's favorite pastimes are reader conventions, traveling, shopping and reading.

She resides in beautiful, small town Georgia with her super-hero husband Kurt and three doggies.

Visit her website at www.hildiemcqueen.com
Facebook: facebook.com/HildieMcQueen
Twitter: twitter.com/HildieMcQueen
Instagram: instagram.com/hildiemcqueenwriter